The Singing Widow
Of A Buddhist Priest

By Ruth Reiner

© *2020 Ruth Reiner* All rights reserved.

All rights reserved. No portion of this book may be reproduced in any form without permission from the publisher, except as permitted by U.S. copyright law.

This is a work of fiction. Names, characters, places, and incidents either are the products of the author's imagination or are used fictitiously. Any resemblance to actual persons, living or dead, businesses, companies, events, or locales is entirely coincidental.

Acknowledgements

I am grateful to my parents for supporting my voyage, which was born from my love of Japan, and their ongoing confidence in me and for simply loving me for who I am. I am grateful for having Ofri, my son and inspiration for this book. Thanks to my siblings for reading a million drafts. Thanks to Rabbi David Rosen and the Honorable Kyotaro Deguchi for inviting me to spend a year in Kyoto with the Oomoto Shinto community. Thanks to all the wonderful people of the Oomoto community, who shared with me their trust, love, and a year of their lives, allowing me to truly experience life in a traditional Japanese society. Thanks to the Hata family, my family in Japan over the years, for always making me feel at home. Thanks to the Japan-America Institute of Management Science and the University of Hawaii, where I received a Japan-focused MBA that allowed me to experience more than ten years of intense work in Japan and with the Japanese. Finally, thanks to the authors, Sagit Emet and Lily Baines, for guidance; to Rebecca DeLancré, for the great book cover; and to both my editors, Nikki Littman and Kristin Campbell. I am so very grateful.

Chapter 1: The Flight

When you travel on business as frequently as I do, you tend to create travel habits to keep you upbeat within your removed and unnatural lifestyle. For one, you become addicted to the concept of visiting the executive lounge between flights. Even the thought of sitting in the terminal hall or waiting at the gate can make you quite edgy. But, in reality, most business lounges are nothing to write home about. The food is usually compatible with the inedible substances served on aircrafts, as if special efforts have been put into creating an authentic, heartburn-triggering, rubber-textured, air-travel-related cuisine culture. If you're there for the booze, well, that—thank God—gets you just the same.

Nasty turbulence!
Ouch! I just banged my head on the window!
No more executive lounge booze for you, Mr. Pilot!

I have been living in Tokyo for the past four years and have just recently helped close one of the biggest transactions my firm has ever landed. I'm the youngest—full disclosure: I'm thirty-seven years old—as well as the first foreigner to become head of division. And I'm certainly the first woman to ever reach an executive position within the one hundred and thirty-six years since my firm was established.

This didn't come easy, to say the least. Whatever could go wrong did go wrong. And I wouldn't be exaggerating if I said, "People almost died." There was also the cultural challenges.

Among other things, I have learned to play golf, but have yet to improve, and worked hard on tolerating excessive amounts of alcohol. Admittedly, the most challenging of all was that I learned to shut my mouth when needed.

By the way, my name is Sarah Green, which is not the easiest name for the Japanese to pronounce, so my colleagues call me "Sala," which, in Japanese, literally means "plate." It would have been nice to have a name that sounded more meaningful in Japanese. Something like—

Ouch! Not again!

Oops! There goes my tonic right on Mr. Kobayashi's sweater.

Oh no! Is that an ice cube sliding down his—

Ooo, what an evil way to wake up!

Stay calm ...

No, I can't be serious! I am not really considering reaching out to his ... Maybe I should try to grab it?

I mean the ice cube!

Okay, the ice cube has reached the point of no return. Don't breathe!

DON'T STARE AT IT! The window! Look out the window!

No, pretend you're reading! No, pretend you're sleeping!

Okay, he is not waking up.
Now, where was I?

When you live in Tokyo, with approximately eleven million other people, it is not difficult to lose yourself both physically and emotionally. The secret for survival is to create a comfort zone around your home; a daily routine in which you recognize your coffee shop, flower shop, convenience store, or any other landmark in your proximity. These landmarks will soon carry that unique DNA that creates your personal habitats. And you can use them to navigate your way back to what you can then call *home*. Then, and only then, when you discover your special path home, the chaos will transform into that unique sense of clarity you desperately need in order to end yet another day in one of the biggest and loneliest metropoles.

My landmarks are on the path leading from my subway station to my apartment building. First, you pass the life-saving 7-Eleven. Next, you reach the pharmacy with the delightful and chatty, always smiling pharmacist, Akiko, who never misses a day of work. And last, but not least, is a small Buddhist temple where Mrs. Toda, the sweet, devoted widow of a Buddhist priest, lives alone with her fluffy, flat-nosed, white Persian cat.

Whenever I pass by the temple during the early hours of the day, I find Mrs. Toda sweeping the pebbles off the path leading from the entrance gate or gently drawing lines through the pebbles in her Zen-style stone garden. In the evenings, however, the sounds from Mrs. Toda's temple and residence are completely different. As a member of a karaoke club, she spends long hours practicing for their weekly singing sessions. Mrs. Toda typically sings one of those old traditional Japanese songs; songs you feel deep nostalgia for, even if you have never heard them before. They are the songs that reflect that romantic flare of Japan that you sometimes come across in those old classic movies. On the coldest of evenings, when I come home late from work, there is something heartwarming about hearing Mrs. Toda's voice as it accompanies me from the temple gate all the way to the entrance of my apartment building.

Not another hit to my head! Again?
Finally! Mr. Kobayashi is awake!
Whoa! Our plane is going down!
Whoops, there goes my hand!

I grab Mr. Kobayashi's hand, and then comes the thought that I have never touched him before, not even by mistake. Not even to shake his hand.

He shows no resistance.

Mr. Kobayashi is my boss. Though deeply intoxicated, it seems he is just as terrified as I am that this flight may not end as he expected.

Panic crawls up my spine. The aircraft dips into another sharp dive. The tension builds up in and around me as people start losing control over what they say and how loud they say it. The cabin crew, the pilot, brief announcements—everything is moving so fast.

I'm paralyzed. And now I'm screaming!

To someone who travels by air so often, there is something almost familiar about an airplane losing control. It is that feeling somewhere in the back of your mind that you have already rehearsed this scene, and now, finally, the curtains have risen and the show has begun. Those moments of uncertainty feel like an eternity. While immense pressure races through your ears and eyes, your heart sinks to your toes, and your hands go numb. At that point—or so I have always imagined—the faces of those who need you and will suffer from your loss appear before your eyes.

Think harder! Think harder! I urge myself, but no faces appear.

I can't breathe.

I unbuckle my seat belt and stand. And then, as if possessed, I yell at the top of my lungs, "*I want a baby!*"

Chapter 2: Where It All Began

I grew up in a standard New Jersey suburb, so insignificant that the only thing we took pride in was our proximity to New York City. Most of the Jewish kids I knew went to Jewish Sunday school where their parents hoped they would learn to read some Hebrew before they finally reached their Bar or Bat Mitzvah ceremony. My parents were no different.

My father, an extremely resourceful individual, strived to educate me by his own life motto: "Do what you need to do." When you knew what was expected from you, the motto implied you should comply. When you had neither clue, guidance, nor explicit expectations set for you, the motto ironically implied: *figure it out for yourself.* Surprisingly or not, "Do what you need to do" suited nearly every situation, and Sunday school was simply one of those things everyone had to do.

My mother, on the other hand, was terrified of the smallest of conflicts, so she found her own way to educate me about taking responsibility for my choices. When I told her that I hated Sunday school and asked that she let me off the hook, she replied in a slightly anxious voice, as if she were being blamed for the weather, that it was an issue between my father and myself.

Imagine being raised by parents who basically believed that their only child somehow needed to figure out what she needed to do by means of the most self-contradicting motto. And that's exactly what led me into countless adventures, to put it lightly!

So, going back to where it all began, just a few months before I turned twelve and was soon to be a Bat Mitzvah girl, my Hebrew teacher, Eli, a former Israel Defense Force soldier, walked into our classroom with a videotape of the movie *Hiroshima Mon Amour* in his hand. It was a black and white movie about a beautiful French woman and a handsome Japanese man who had a love affair in Hiroshima nearly a decade after the Second World War. Their love affair was set against a city that had suffered horror and devastation and had been built upon inhumane ruins.

That movie left an immense impression on me. In my eyes, it portrayed the essence of true romance—a mixture of passion, trauma, and despair, pulling and tearing these strangers from the inside while, at the same time, they are wrapped in each other's arms.

Though I was never French, trauma, despair, and passion did find their way into my major relationships. But let's keep that for later.

The stories of the A-bomb and its victims wove in and out of the dialogues between the handsome Japanese doctor and the shattered but graceful French nurse. Together, with the horrifying snapshots from the war and its aftermath, somehow, all that pain and suffering around them and within them was contained within their passionate romance. The movie left the twelve-year-old me feeling both significantly overwhelmed as well as ironically full of hope. Hope that someday someone would hold me in his arms and help me contain all my darkest and greatest fears.

Right up to the end of the movie, we still had no idea why Eli would choose to show us a French-Japanese movie as part of his once-a-week Hebrew language lesson. As the credits rolled, he got up from his seat, turned on the classroom lights, and opened the shades.

My heartbeat accelerated as tension, mixed with the excitement of hearing Eli's voice and catching his soft gaze, took over.

Pushing back his long, curly hair and uncovering his light green, hypnotic eyes, he scanned our faces slowly. Then, in his soft voice and strong Hebrew accent, he stated, "I was meant to discuss the Holocaust with you today. However, sometimes I feel that we see ourselves as the sole victims of that war." He paused, looking carefully at each and every one of us. "We sometimes forget our role in demonstrating compassion for the suffering of others."

As these words came out of his mouth, my mouth dried and my eyes watered.

The room was more silent in that moment than it ever had been. That was ... until suddenly the TV screen went fuzzy and a sharp noise shifted our attention from Eli to the TV.

Before Eli could even consider moving toward it to turn it off, Naomi, the energetic redhead who had sat next to me from the first day of Sunday school and my best friend, sprinted like a roadrunner across the room, hit the power button and, within a split-second, was back in her seat.

Eli had lost his train of thought as his gaze followed Naomi across the room from her seat to the TV and back. And, as soon as she had turned the TV off, there was complete silence again. Then, just as Eli detached his eyes from Naomi and shared his glossy gaze with the rest of us, and just before he could say another word, the bell rang!

The tension broke, and then everyone was out the door. Mothers waited in the hallway, consumed with that Jewish mother's guilt for sending us to school on Sunday and determined to make it up to us by spoiling us rotten for the remaining hours of the weekend.

Eli silently collected his belongings and left the classroom, sending a quick glimpse and lonely smile in my direction. I was the only one still at my desk. He then headed out into the noisy hall with his hair hanging heavy over his shoulders.

I felt I was the only one who was truly sympathetic toward Eli's silent withdrawal from the one lesson that he seemed sincerely passionate to pass on to us. His last words, "We sometimes forget our role," kept resonating in my head the following week.

Unfortunately, some parents found Eli's comparison of A-bomb victims to the Holocaust victims outrageous and had him fired before our next class. Rumor had it that, shortly after he was fired, he returned to Israel and, a few years later, opened a small sushi bar in southern Tel Aviv with a big sign at its entrance that read: "*DON'T FORGET YOUR ROLE!*"

Chapter 3: Finding My Role!

It wasn't until I turned twenty-four that I truly felt it was time for me to take charge and fulfill *my role*. It was Thanksgiving weekend, and Naomi and I had scheduled to meet up, as we did on all major holidays while visiting our parents back in New Jersey.

In Jewish Sunday school, most kids only noticed the fact that Naomi was always the first to take charge and often thought she was arrogant. I thought it was pretty cool to have a friend with such sharp instincts. I even saw her as having some sort of super power. I admit, I did sometimes envy the way she roamed the world with such a solid sense of confidence, as if she never needed anyone to tell her to *do what she needed to do*, as if she never doubted what that "right thing to do" was.

That particular Thanksgiving was special because it was the first time Naomi and I had seen each other since she had officially become a firefighter.

In our community, her career choice was—to put it softly—"frowned upon" and rather inappropriate for a nice Jewish girl, especially one with her Ivy League credentials.

Naomi, however, was Naomi. She was bulletproof. True, she had already learned to ignore the gossip, but this was nothing compared to what she had gone through when she had decided to bring her hot Asian-American college grad girlfriend, Alysa, as her date to her high school prom. Remember, we are talking about the early 1990s.

Keeping true to her superhero nature, she appeared perfectly content with her career choice. I personally thought it was an excellent choice for her, being the hyperactive, redheaded, women's rights advocate pistol she was. And no less, a true win for humanity.

Naomi and I met at one of the very few good sushi hangouts on our side of the Hudson River. We spent the better part of our lunch laughing at her colorful, mega-heroic stories. My life seemed uneventful compared to hers—dull and leading nowhere. I simply *did what I needed to do*. I had earned my undergraduate degree in liberal arts from NYU, had done some light, conventional European travel, but found nothing that really made me tick.

After a few rounds of saké and enough sushi to fill three Thanksgiving turkeys, I went to wash the remaining fumes of wasabi off my hands when *it* happened.

Outside the restroom was a sign.

Yes, literally a sign—*my* sign.

SPEND A YEAR IN HIROSHIMA!
An educational foundation in Hiroshima is
seeking a university graduate. The position
includes assisting local staff with
international communications, events, and

publications. The appropriate candidate must be friendly and polite, with a keen interest in Japanese culture ...

A postal address for submitting applications was plastered on the bottom of the sign. The mailing address was in Japan.

I stood there and read the sign again and again. Finally, as if overtaken by a force greater than me, I removed the sign from the billboard, feeling that I had finally reached a defining moment in my life.

Now what? I asked myself, holding my undeniable destiny in my hands.

I stood there another moment, half-anxious and half-thrilled.

Perhaps one of the Japanese workers here knows more about it, I thought, sliding the omen under my jacket and walking back toward the main dining area.

Everyone seemed profoundly busy, and I didn't know whom to turn to. Then I noticed the Japanese woman at the cash register and somehow concluded that she looked the most informed. Maybe it was her large retro glasses or her curly, salt and pepper hair shoved under an old-fashioned hair net. I don't know.

I took a deep breath, leveled my chin, and with a nice, polite smile on my face, I walked toward her. Then, standing in front of her, I flashed the sign from under my jacket. "I think this is my role!" I whispered to her, pointing at it with one hand.

But the woman at the cash register simply stared back at

me with blank eyes.

I waited for her to finally say something then simply figured:

a) She did not understand English;

b) She was shocked by my subtle vandalism/kleptomania; or

c) She expected a "university graduate" to be younger (truth be told, a few years had passed since I had graduated).

After what seemed like a very long game of *Who Blinks First*, she finally lost. I was relieved and assumed she had finally registered what I had said.

"Sushi roll?" she asked in an unexpected, fairly high-pitched voice and with a courteous smile.

My hands were clammy as I took a deep breath and finally said, "Yes, I want to pay for our sushi rolls."

The woman smiled back and tilted her head slightly, her eyes refusing to blink again.

I turned toward our table to get my purse then realized Naomi, as usual, had beaten me to it.

That same night at my parents' home, when everyone finally retired to bed, I sat down to prepare my application letter. On the following Monday morning, I sent the letter to Japan. A few months—and several rainforests worth of paperwork later—my life finally took an unprecedented twist, and I was on my way to Hiroshima, Japan.

Chapter 4: When An Alien Lands

I first traveled to Japan in 1998. What I remember the most, when first landing there and gazing at the fellow passengers around me, stepping off the plane, was how the Japanese women, without exception, appeared invigorated. It had been a very long flight, and I, for one, felt like nothing less than a deflated furry animal. Actually, I didn't just feel like one. I took a short detour to the restroom for a quick damage control analysis in front of the mirror and swore I kind of looked like one.

My hair was as flat as it gets and lost all willingness to revive. I tried to force it, yet my fluffing it from side to side made no difference. My face was pale but not in a proper Geisha painted way. I had never been good at traveling with a set of makeup, so I managed the situation the old-fashioned way—with a few slaps to my cheeks, I recovered some color to my face. I smiled at all the intense eyes fixed on their own already perfected faces and hoped they had missed my freakshow. Then I headed toward passport control.

At passport control, I was diverted to the "Aliens Only" line. The Japanese's choice of English words puzzled me sometimes.

At the aliens' line, I found myself standing behind a tall, Swedish guy, accompanied by a thin and even taller, elastic-looking, icy-blue, bright-eyed woman. I entertained myself with the thought that only the Japanese could expect aliens to go through passport control, and then I thought that the Swedish couple could definitely pass for aliens.

After only a few suspicious looks from the border control officer, and an unreciprocated smile from my end, I was on my way to the baggage claim where my two overloaded suitcases were already waiting there, just on time to carry my past into the future. Having said that, I had never anticipated that getting them on the luggage cart would be my first authentic, cross-cultural lesson. Putting it gently, I soon found myself battling again and again to hold, lift, swing, and place my massive suitcases on the baggage cart. The cart just kept rolling away! Yes, a world without baggage cart brakes, for real! 1998. Then I started to perspire, and my post-slapped cheeks turned a crimson red.

I was ready to yell at the top of my lungs. My desperate attempts seemed useless. I felt I had no choice. So, I broke. I dropped the luggage on the floor and emitted a squeal of distress into the universe. It was the only non-mechanical sound within my immediate radius, and though I had no doubt there wasn't a single soul in baggage claim who was not aware of my desperation, no one even blinked in my direction.

It became clear to me that I could have been buried under my suitcases and left to die, and no one would have jumped to my rescue. As it turned out, being spared the embarrassment of knowing that others *had* noticed how clumsy, sweaty, and helpless I was, somehow, in their world, it made their avoidance the noble thing to do.

"Finally, I got you!" I found myself shouting out with a slight tone of victory, in spite of my ungrateful suitcases. Then, sweaty but ready, I pushed my hair back and strolled into the Arrivals Hall of Kansai Airport. *Katano-san*, I reminded myself of the name of the man who was meant to collect me.

Running my eyes over dozens of identical, expressionless faces, I stood there, scanning the terrain until a chubby, anxious man finally materialized in front of me and asked, "Sala-san?"

"Yes. Hello," I answered with a big smile. "Or should I say *konichiwa*?" I quickly added in the sweetest voice I could manage. "Katano-san, right?" I finally concluded, noticing his mind was already elsewhere.

"*Hai*," he replied.

Knowing that *hai* meant *yes* boosted my confidence instantly. I wasn't willing to turn out totally clueless, amid all my other flops at the airport.

I opened my mouth to continue with some greetings, using the few Japanese sentences I had been practicing for the last several weeks and on the plane, but he instantly cut me off with a strict and severe tone, stating that our train was to leave in four minutes.

Shocked, jet-lagged, and totally disoriented, I found myself chasing after a middle-aged Japanese man, dragging behind me two massive suitcases and a diluted shadow.

Mr. Katano was my boss's translator and had been my main point of contact during the application period. We had mostly exchanged letters, but there had been two short phone conversations, as well. When we had spoken over the phone, he had seemed quite friendly. He'd had an awkward giggle, which reminded me of Goofy, the Walt Disney character. I was, therefore, quite surprised when his compact, chubby stature turned out to emit all but friendliness and was more like a French bulldog.

As I got to know Mr. Katano, I realized that, if I were to sum up his personality in Asian-flavored words, I would describe him as a sweet and sour individual, depending on the percentage of alcohol in his blood at any given time of day. No alcohol equaled low tolerance without exceptions. The day I had arrived, he had apparently purchased return train tickets to Hiroshima set for a specific time without considering it might take me longer than he had expected to clear customs and collect my luggage. It turned out that he simply wanted to make sure he got back to the office in time for the division's after-work alcohol and snacks gathering.

Despite the hustle, and without the slightest assistance from Mr. Katano, we reached our train on time. Let's not even talk about my physical appearance again. It. Was. Bad.

Mr. Katano exchanged very few words with me on the way to Hiroshima, seeming to prefer a long nap. And during the transits, he simply scurried as fast as possible to catch the earliest connection. He projected a sense of urgency, which could not be overlooked. He was so determined to make it back to Hiroshima on time that he hardly turned back to see whether I, carrying a year's worth of possessions, had even caught up.

Well, I hardly had. Not by a long shot.

I would never forget that first train ride in Japan. I had imagined the country as a never-ending mass of ultramodern, overcrowded cities, where nature was both suppressed and compressed into bonsai tree dimensions. I was, therefore, surprised to discover that Japan was more countryside than metropolis—a green, hilly landscape of volcanic islands.

I should note here that the Japanese believe that the spirits of the dead reside on the mountaintops, and so construction in the countryside is therefore restricted to narrow strips of land between the highlands and the subsiding rice fields. In these residential patches, compact homes are lined up like mazes, complemented by miniature-sized cars with big Japanese brand names.

We finally reached Hiroshima's central station. Once we exited the platforms and headed toward the front gate, it was as if the race had ended. Mr. Katano asked me to wait with my belongings and detoured toward the local payphone to make a call. I stretched a bit then took my first deep breath, exhaling some of the anxiety that I had been harboring since landing.

Looking around, I thought, *I could live here*. There was just something so different and odd yet almost naïve about the setting. Everything seemed tiny and tangible, almost like a set built on a miniature golf course. I felt a bit like Alice in Wonderland. It was as if, after chasing the rabbit, either I grew into oversized clumsy dimensions, or everything shrank around me.

I am not sure how long I stood there, staring past Mr. Katano, before realizing he had returned from his call. By the tone of his voice, I assumed he had called my name more than once. He pointed toward the streetcar and continued pacing ahead of me, signaling to me to follow.

After a few stops on the streetcar, which moved quite slow yet smoothly, we reached our station that was just in front of the employee housing. Although the structure seemed like a plain, generic office building on the outside, when entering, I instantly experienced the clash of civilizations as the traditional Japanese met the modern, miraculously blending together.

The woman at the reception counter, Hiroko-san, who could probably have passed as Mr. Katano's mother, scurried diligently toward the front door in small, confined steps, restrained by her tight Kimono. Opening the door as we arrived, she then bowed again and again, smiling and repeating the word "welcome" as many times as she could manage until we all reached the reception. She was exceptionally friendly, which was a relief—I guess Mr. Katano's attitude had started getting to me. After all, our journey from the airport was not how I had imagined it after a long, exhausting flight.

Hiroko-san spoke very little English but had soft features and a reassuring smile. She handed me a pair of slippers and, without hesitation, placed my shoes on one of the many unoccupied shelves near the entrance as I put on the slippers. Then she picked up one of my suitcases, carrying it effortlessly toward the staircase. It struck me with surprise, both her strength as well as the fact that she was the first person to lend me a hand since I had arrived in Japan. *She would have probably placed the baggage on the God-awful luggage cart seamlessly, as well.* I was amused by the thought.

I grabbed the other suitcase, somehow managing to

gather just enough strength to head up the staircase and down the corridor behind her. Meanwhile, I noticed that Mr. Katano quickly made his way to the door, mumbling something about being in touch in a few days, once I got some rest. Then he vanished behind the glass door.

My first few days in Hiroshima were a blur. I experienced both acute jet lag and an overwhelming culture shock. I tried to distinguish between new tastes, odd smells, and green teas. My one-room suite was as compact as everything else in the country seemed to be. My bathroom had a soft pink, insulated toilet seat and a showerhead that reached only as high as my shoulders, forcing me to kneel every time I washed my hair. Sleeping on a futon mattress on the tatami floor was a challenge, since my front was not familiar with hard surfaces. Morning became night and dusk became dawn. As a result, I hardly met a soul, other than when I actually got up in time to catch a meal at the employee dining room. When I did come across someone in the hallway, he or she would either pretend not to notice me, or greet me briefly in Japanese and instantly retire beyond sight.

Mr. Katano called two days later, announcing, without pause, that he would pick me up the next day at 7:30 a.m. and take me to the office. As expected, he hung up before I had the chance to respond.

The next day, I wore my best clothes, and although I went down to the lobby five minutes early, I found Mr. Katano already waiting.

The office building was a short walk from the employee housing and was typically 80s in style. It was three stories with grayish-blue, wall-to-wall carpeting, smelling of dampness that resembled many other office buildings I have visited ever since in Japan. At the entrance to our office were grey lockers, just like the ones I had back in high school.

As we stepped into what seemed like a randomly divided space, silence took over. Well, everyone went silent except for one individual. That person was talking on the phone, or more like monologuing to the handset, bowing extensively to the person on the other end of the line, regardless of the fact that the other person was out of sight. That individual was Mr. Odo, head of our division.

Mr. Odo was exceptionally polite and looked kind of like Kevin Spacey ... Well, in the same way that, some years later, Japanese Prime Minister Koizumi looked to many like a Japanese version of Richard Gere.

From the moment I was officially introduced to my office colleagues, people in the employee housing seemed friendlier, as well.

During my time there, I did what I was asked to do, trying my best to fit into an unfamiliar dynamic built on codes that I was constantly hoping to crack. I edited translated stories of A-Bomb survivors, received foreign dignitaries, and even helped plan a medium-scale international event. But, at times, I felt that Mr. Odo didn't expect much of me, and I wished I had been treated like the others ... I should say treated like the rest of my *male* colleagues, being one of three women among more than twenty employees in the division.

Mrs. Takahashi was the oldest female in our division. She was probably in her fifties, maintained a very motherly attitude, and was always attired quite modestly. Except for serving tea and coffee, she was not expected to take part in any meetings concerning real content. Yet, she seemed content with her role.

At the other end of the age range was Noriko-chan. She was a recent university graduate, smart, spirited, very outspoken, and always dressed as a Japanese Barbie on her way to meet the Japanese Ken. Although she was only twenty-two and had been hired to assist Mrs. Takahashi, she seemed to have greater aspirations than being an *OL*—the Japanese abbreviation for "Office Lady," in contrast to "Salary Men," the typical name for white-collared male employees. I was sure that Noriko-chan frequently outsmarted our male colleagues, but that seemed irrelevant. Everyone treated her below her capabilities and aspirations, like a lovable twelve-year-old who was simply seeking attention.

Noriko-chan and I had our own channel of communications. It started with her parents asking me to tutor her in English. Then, before I knew it, they had adopted me as Noriko's older sister and had approached me with the expectation that I would help prepare their daughter in becoming a worthy Japanese wife. I honestly couldn't tell you why they would choose *me* to prepare her in becoming what I could never be. They knew that she had a lust for life behind her girlish appearance yet hoped I would help contain it within the norms. Nonetheless, for some odd reason, my presence in her life seemed to have given them more confidence in her.

On her end, Noriko had me join her for parties with friends, shopping crazes, and shared her wildest dreams with me. She dreamt of being as free to become whomever she wanted to be, just as she felt I had. She gave me a window into a part of me that had not lived to the extent that she had when

I had been her age. I had traveled and had my university years, but I never had her thirst for life.

I loved every moment I shared with her. She became the sister I never had. She helped me balance the dull, male-dominated, after-office drink sessions with uncensored escapism. She exposed me to the lives of a generation of Japanese who no longer believed in lifetime employment, nor in the gender roles so deeply engraved in the minds of the elders.

During the first few months of my year in Hiroshima, I would occasionally leave the office in the evenings and head out to the busy post-office-hour streets, scanning the herd for Eli. I somehow imagined he would be there, waiting for me, his first words being, "You never forgot your role!"

I felt indeed that I was fulfilling my role—that role of opening my heart to the suffering of others. Meetings with A-bomb victims had opened me to so many parts of my soul, but what hit me the strongest was the fact that, despite having survived the horror of being victims to an atomic bombing, they were able, through their unique, culturally enhanced views on life, to find peace within them, empathy, humility, and a great desire to live.

Every meeting began with them presenting me with a small gift—usually, a local sweet of some sort. Some asked me to visit them again, to meet their families. Some families invited me to day trips to local shrines or even to magical Onsens—public baths in breathtaking, natural surroundings. Their thirst to host me with open hearts was a humbling experience, to say the least, which made me ever more curious as to how their approach to me as an American could be so unconditional. I was thankful for Eli for opening this window into my soul.

Yet, I could not deny the fact that there were days when I would feel lonely, wanting to comfort myself. I would even go further and imagine how Eli and I would meet at the Hiroshima Peace Memorial Park, staring at the remains of the dome, the skies covered with the reds of a lustful sunset. We would then start a passionate love affair, just like the Japanese doctor and French nurse in *Hiroshima Mon Amour*.

I never did bump into Eli, and I doubted he would have recognized me if we would have met. After all, the last time he had seen me, I was half my age.

It took a few months before I got used to my new work routine with the backdrop scenery of a 1980's office and my modest accommodations. The more I came to know the locals, the more I was determined to be exactly what the position on the sign had required—friendly, polite, and unquestionably interested in Japanese culture.

Chapter 5: Old Christmas Cake

On the morning of my twenty-fifth birthday, just a few months after arriving in Hiroshima, I woke up to the most spectacular bouquet of flowers. With the flowers came a note that read, "*Happy birthday! See you this evening!*" At the bottom of the note was a round stamp with a signature. It was the stamp that the Japanese used to sign their names, but I could not recall any of my colleagues who would use these Japanese characters, so I had no idea who the bouquet was from.

As soon as I arrived at the office, Mr. Odo called out from his desk, "Sala-san! *O-tanjobi omedetou gozaimasu!*"

Mr. Katano, who scanned the newspaper on his desk with his eyes half-shut, instantly raised his head and hurried to translate, "Happy birthday, Sala!"

After that, more and more colleagues rose from their seats to greet me one by one. By the time I reached my desk, my cheeks burned. I was overwhelmed by the massive attack of greetings.

Mr. Katano stood in front of me at my desk, even before I had the chance to pull my chair in and take a breath of relief.

He looked down at me with his tiny, hungover eyes, searching for words. Then he finally declared, "Odo-Sensei and his wife would like you to join them for a dinner party this evening at their home." He paused, and I could see he was striving to remember the rest of the details. "Oh ... for your birthday," he finally added.

"I would be honored," I answered, flattered and deeply surprised, as I had never thought I would be so privileged as to visit him at his home.

Mr. Katano bowed his head slightly in approval then drifted away toward Mr. Odo's desk where I could hear their dialogue continue.

Before leaving the office, Mr. Katano asked me to meet him at 6:00 p.m. in front of the flower shop at the station closest to Mr. Odo's home.

As soon as we met at the station, I saw Mr. Katano's face, and I could tell that he had something he wanted to say, something he had no idea how to break to me. It was the same expression he had worn the time he had asked me which method of birth control I used. He had evidently read that Japanese women couldn't use the pill, due to the fact that their brain was structured differently, and he was just wondering if I had one of those unique brain structures that could survive the hormonal intrusion. Seems legit, right?

Another time, with that same expression on his face, he had asked me why Princess Diana was not loyal to her husband, as if, being an English-speaking foreign woman granted me some unique insight into the souls and roles of the royal British family.

As we started walking toward the Odos' residence, Mr.

Katano continued to search for words until he finally opened with, "In Japan, Christmas Eve is celebrated with a Christmas cake—a white cream cake—not with a Christmas tree …"

I halted and eyed him quizzically, realizing that this conversation might be even odder than I had expected. On the one hand, I thought to myself, *Why would he mention Christmas in March?* On the other hand, *A cake instead of a tree made perfect sense to me. After all, it is the celebration of Christ's birthday.* Being raised Jewish and all, I wouldn't have done either.

Though less than one percent of Japanese are Christians, I learned to accept the fact that any gift exchange opportunity is welcomed in Japan. And thus, Christmas seemed to meet the criteria. However, the tree was another story altogether, since Japanese homes are too small for trees. So, in short, it seemed like a fair tradeoff to go for a cream cake.

Back to Mr. Katano, his cadence increased in that awkward way he trot-walked, and without looking back at me, he continued, "In Japan, when a woman is not married by the age of twenty-five, she is, you know, like an old Christmas cake."

Admittedly, it took me a few seconds to understand the relevance of his Christmas story to our lives. But Mr. Katano wasn't finished.

"When Odo-Sensei heard you were turning twenty-five, he got a bit worried. You understand?"

Before I could even think of reacting in any way, Mr. Katano quickly noted that we had arrived at the Odo residence. In fact, Mrs. Odo was just in front of us, waiting at the entrance to their home, a welcoming smile on her face, wearing a magically colorful kimono.

Mr. Katano and I bowed several times as he recited an extensive series of greetings to our hostess and boss's wife. I was still speechless by his somewhat displaced prologue but managed to keep a smile on my face as I followed his lead regarding the expected rituals, greetings, and bows.

Next, we were seated at a small wooden bench in the entrance to their home, where we could comfortably remove our shoes while Mrs. Odo gently and gracefully laid slippers at our feet. With our slippers on, we then followed her as she soundlessly glided in her kimono through the narrow halls of their home.

At the end of the hall, traditional Japanese translucent doors spanned the space. Mrs. Odo removed her slippers, knelt, and then slid open the doors. We removed our slippers, as well, bowed at the doorway on our knees, and then quietly entered the traditional Japanese room.

Mr. Odo was seated atop a cushion on the tatami floor in front of a long, dark, knee-high wooden table. Across from Mr. Odo sat an unfamiliar Japanese man. They were both enjoying the view of a spectacular, well-lit garden, visible from beyond an additional set of sliding doors across from the main entrance.

Mrs. Odo seated me in my appointed place next to the unknown man, then Mr. Odo introduced me to him. Mr. Katano quickly translated his words.

I failed to catch his full name, but it triggered a memory of one of the Japanese characters from the round signature at the bottom of the note attached to the bouquet of flowers that I had received that morning.

The man, who had been introduced to me as a successful doctor, nodded as a sign of humility and waved his hand in denial, as culturally expected. He must have been about ten years older than me. I'd heard that it was not uncommon for successful Japanese men in their mid-thirties, particularly doctors, to still be single, unlike women, of course. However, I was both touched and a little self-conscious that my boss, determined to spare me the shame of being an "old Christmas cake," thoughtfully but without even considering preparing me for this, fished out a doctor for me from the great ocean of lonely Japanese souls. Must had figured out most Jewish women wanted to marry doctors, or at least their mothers were sure to approve.

The evening was colorful, packed with unique flavors and smells. My boss's wife, still wrapped elegantly in her tasteful kimono, served a ten-course meal that included homemade tempura lightly fried before our eyes by Mr. Odo himself. The food was delicious, and no bite tasted like the other.

From time to time, I made subtle eye contact with the doctor, who constantly complimented the Odos on their cooking. Something about my blind date made me envision him as a sort of Japanese Clark Kent. I could give him the benefit of the doubt that, in some parallel universe, perhaps he had a wild Superman side to him. He was exceptionally tall for a Japanese and well-built by all standards. But his superhero, perhaps even super-lover, attributes were simply hidden too deeply behind the geekiest eyeglasses and hairstyle I had come across for some time.

As we finished the main course and thanked our hosts

once again for the sumptuous feast, my flower-delivering, nerdy-Superman-resembling, mysterious doctor finally gathered the courage to turn my way and ask, "So, what do you think about the American erections?"

I have to hand it to Dr. Kent; he must have spent the better part of the evening practicing this opening line in his head.

The Odos watched me keenly, anticipating my reply to a question that they did not even understand, as it was in English—or at least was intended to be. They were undoubtedly curious as to how I would handle myself with the man who they hoped would bite into my almost outdated cream cake.

Before I could say a word, Mr. Odo repeated in a questioning tone, "American erections?" He said it in the way the Japanese have the tendency of repeating words they do not understand, since Mr. Katano, anticipating my reaction together with the others, had forgotten to translate.

Mr. Katano then jumped right in to explain, having been caught off guard. Finally, the Odos answered with an "Aaah!"

Mrs. Odo then decided to repeat the words herself to make sure she had gotten it right. "American erections," she said, demonstrating her understanding of the new phrase she had just learned.

Finally, all eyes were on me again, eager for my response.

I tried to avoid eye contact with Mr. Katano; I couldn't imagine that he hadn't heard what I had heard when they all made the often fatal Japanese error of exchanging the "L" with an "R."

I carefully swallowed the remainder of my tea, put on my sophisticated look—the one where my eyebrows elevate to the top of my forehead—and dove into U.S. Politics 101, saving myself from the overwhelming desire to blow his horn. No pun intended. However, it was one of those *do what you need to do* situations, so I ditched the "L/R" controversy and simply dug in.

All in all, I have always loved even those cheesy, awkward Japanese situations. And while falling asleep that night, I actually felt grateful for Mr. Odo's concern. I could not recall the last time my parents had concerned themselves with my personal life, let alone my love life. It was even kind of comforting, as if Mr. Odo was hoping to provide me with some parental guidance, something I might have lacked in my "individualistic upbringing" environment. Nonetheless, lacking parental guidance or not, I was not ready to comply.

The next morning, when I got to the office, I informed Mr. Katano that I was thankful for the Odos' kind gesture; however, I was living my dream simply by sharing the window into souls of so many inspiring individuals, questioning my norms and paradigm against those of a culture that was just starting to unfold before my eyes. I had no desire whatsoever to settle down.

I could not say that Mr. Katano seemed surprised, though he did seem a bit lost in translation, or at least lost in a world where Christmas cakes had an impact on social norms. I think that was the first instance I actually felt some sort of sympathy toward him. He was a bridge of sorts—perhaps a rope bridge for me—trying to connect Venus and Mars as I stepped into outer space, an alien in Japan.

That day, I realized I was totally in love, not with one single Japanese individual but rather with the Japanese people as a whole. It was something about the fact that I knew their hearts were in the right place, yet they challenged my imagination in their desire to communicate their sincerity. I felt as if I was the luckiest person alive to have had the chance to explore such a different world that constantly defied my expectations. I was alive and kicking, relentlessly excited to tie my life to Japan, but not with any one particular soul. At least, not in the foreseeable future.

Chapter 6: Every End Is A New Beginning

When my year in Hiroshima ended, I inevitably returned home. Well, figuratively, I returned. Emotionally, I felt a part of me hadn't. It was as if I had left my colorful life in Oz, following the yellow brick road, overcoming new challenges each day, and after a "click of my heels," I had landed back in a black and white, nothing-ever-changes. The only thing that made sense to me was that I had to find my way back to Japan.

My deepest revelation, however, was that, this time, I would need to have a contingency plan; a way to build a base on my own in Japan, financially independent and without a time limit. Then I understood that my rendezvous must be in a business suit and all it implied. That got me started on building a career with the intention of returning to Japan. I earned a Master's in Business, majoring in Japanese Economy, and then I got a job in foreign exchange trading, where I built up my expertise in the Asian financial markets.

I followed the financial sections of three major Japanese newspapers on a daily basis and knew every Japanese trading house and its cross-shareholdings. I tracked the Nikkei stock exchange daily and tried on dozens of suits, all so I would be prepared for my first official business trip to Japan. At the same time, I did all I could to improve my Japanese language skills. I traveled back and forth to Japan under any pretext—judo competitions, aikido competitions, kendo competitions, koto lessons, kabuki lessons, origami lessons, English teaching, summer holidays, winter getaways, maple leaf and cherry blossom viewings. So, naturally, when I finally came home with Ben, "a nice Jewish boy," and not with a member of the Yakuza, my parents did not take it as a given, though they seemed relieved.

Ben was the first guy I had ever kissed with my chin pointing upward. That is, the first guy I dated who was taller than me. A great kisser; that I have to admit. Ben could easily pass for the model in one of those frames in the photo printing shop. Oh, and he definitely had the most perfect toes I'd ever seen (I am not just saying that; I truly know men's toes! It is a big issue among the men in my father's family.). He had piercing black eyes and very thin lips. Thin lips, by the way, did not put any constraints on the amount of gossip they could generate, at least not in the case of Ben's mother. He also had very thick brown hair, which was always brushed over his forehead and ears—kind of early Justin Bieber, and that was when he was … what? About twelve?

Yet, in Ben's defense, at least he had hair on his head. I had read that men who had more hair on their heads and less on their bodies tended to have less testosterone than those with the opposite combination. In Ben's case, it kind of made sense. Testosterone was not really what I sensed in Ben's presence. He was more the metrosexual type. He could spend hours checking out aftershaves and body lotions at the duty-free shops. For me, this kind of clashed with his wannabe, earthy, simple life kind of guy self-perception. But who was I to judge? Compared to him, I had a six-minutes-max tolerance for duty-free shopping, and I usually ended up with a bottle of gin and a pack of mini Mars Bars if I was in a really intense shopping mood.

Last but not least, Ben had a scar on the left side of his neck. Apparently, he had gotten it on the night of his high school prom. After debating the entire year how to invite a girl named Debby to be his date, he had finally managed, and she had agreed. That, however, had been the first and last conversation they had ever had. On prom night, Ben had tried ironing his collar with his shirt already on, hoping to save time. If that wasn't sad, it could have been funny. Once his mother had seen the long, red scar on Ben's neck, she had begun making hysterical phone calls to any doctor she had listed in her phone book. Ben, in turn, had been forced to stay home until she was confident that he was out of harm's way. Debby had ended up attending the prom on her own, and shame had prevented them both from ever saying a word to one another again. All that, however, hadn't kept me from loving him. The scar was not only physical, it was so much more for the good and for the worse. Knowing the story behind it helped me see his vulnerabilities and helped me share mine.

Ben and I had met in front of an exhibit of an old tribal canoe at Taipei Airport. He had been on his way back home from a "self-discovery mission" across China, and I had been returning from an international ikebana competition in Nagoya where, obviously, I had failed the pre-selection. Ben had asked me if I knew anything about the aboriginal tribes that had once inhabited Taiwan. I had replied that I had no idea there were ever Aborigines in Taiwan, but admittedly still showed very little interest. He had then tried dragging me into a discussion on the relations between China and Taiwan, but here, too, I had showed very little interest. Finally, he had asked where I had flown in from and thus got me to reveal my minor obsession with Japan. Before I could control it, I had shared with him my plans to return one day to the land of the rising sun in a business suit. He had found my fixation somewhat amusing, and I had found his amusement quite flattering, especially considering that, just a few years ago, I had felt like a woman without a story. His plans have always been much more modest.

He imagined himself living on a small farm, growing some crops, maybe raising some cattle, and perhaps writing some short stories in his spare time.

"Something simple," he had explained.

Two years after Ben and I had met at Taipei Airport, we got married. Then, two years later, I was offered the position of analyst at a Japanese firm based in Tokyo. I was thrilled! He was supportive. We were one of those couples.

The time had come, and I was to reappear in the land of the rising sun in my well-chosen, multi-shade suit. By then, of course, there were quite a few suits hanging in my closet. Ben was proud of me and, although he had always claimed he could be content with very little, he was no less psyched to relocate. I had painted his imagination with stories of the great metropolis, and he was ready to cross the Pacific and conquer it.

Soon after I accepted the offer, Ben and I moved to Tokyo. We rented a compact yet highly functional apartment in a building just three stops from Shinjuku station, through which more than four million people passed each day—the furthest one could possibly get from life on a farm.

Chapter 7: A White Carpet

The first month in Japan, Ben and I enjoyed a second honeymoon. Our energies were so high that we couldn't stay apart. We visited the most exquisite hot springs, bathed with monkeys, hit the noisiest pachinko parlors, went shrine hopping on the island of Shikoku, ate twelve different types of tofu at a temple restaurant in Kyoto, and even checked out Tokyo's Disneyland to fulfill Ben's childhood dream, which he had never gotten to fulfill back in the States. I loved every part of our journey together through the magical atmosphere of Japan, that even in a one to one copy of Disneyland, the all-American-brand still stood out.

Japan was in the details. In the softness in which the Japanese interacted with their surroundings, creating harmony with nearly everything. Kind of like *origami* paper that could have various designs—naïve, colorful, and so different than the next, yet would be appreciated just as much, even when matched together. Our love grew and made us feel stronger than ever, yet our dependance and the realization that it was only us against the world grew even stronger.

Within our second month in Japan, tension started to

grow. As I began working full-time, the spark in Ben's eyes began to fade. By the end of the first week of our third month—yes, I remember those days too well—I could not imagine going back home to Ben and his draining state of mind. His loneliness and isolation made him bitter, and he seemed to not be able to master the strength to create his own routine, thus he became fully consumed in challenging mine.

Those days, once I got home, our flat seemed constantly shrinking, and the air seemed thinner and thinner. I started treating myself with shopping therapy—the most accessible type of therapy in Japan. My six-minute tolerance to duty-free shops was history. I stared at rows of lipstick and nail polish for hours. Shopping was the only thing I could think of when my work days ended.

Just a minor detour, I told myself on one of those predetermined, harsh evenings, trying to push away the guilt-ridden images of Ben alone and tormented, which kept intruding on my serenity-seeking conscience. Finally, I converted my guilt into a practical resolution by vowing to buy Ben's forgiveness in return for staying out on the crowded streets and not rushing home.

As I walked through the small side aisles of Tokyo's main shopping grounds, I felt my energy return with the sight of endless merchandise—all colorful, perfectly exhibited, and so appealing. First, I considered buying Ben a pet piranha. Yes, one of those meat-eating fish, though I'm not sure why … Then I thought of buying him a Sony PlayStation, which I imagined would keep him busy for at least the next five years. Next was a huge, perfectly round, eighteen-ounce apple placed on a velvet pillow in a fancy box costing nearly one hundred dollars, giving him something odd yet real to write home about. Finally, I decided to keep it simple and go for something nice for our apartment, something we could both enjoy together.

As I moved in the direction of the interior design shops, I was drawn to it like a moth to a flame. It was the most comforting, soothing, fluffy, inviting white carpet I had ever seen! The moment I saw it, I knew I had to have it. It cost a whole month's salary, but images of a beleaguered Ben instantly transformed into visions of the two of us rolling back and forth on the carpet's white, fluffy perfection, happy as kids making angels in the snow. It warmed my heart, and I was convinced.

The subway ride home with the rolled-up carpet was a challenge, but it was nothing compared to the unexpected welcoming awaiting me at home. I had hoped my soft, furry gift would raise his spirits at least a few inches from the floor.

I entered our flat and called out to Ben, asking him to sit on the sofa and close his eyes. As Ben was already seated on the sofa, I assumed his eyes were closed. Then, hugging it with excitement, I dragged the carpet in from the entrance hall and spread it at Ben's feet. What came next was how I imagined a hero's fall from grace.

Ben was not only extremely upset by my surprise, he also expressed a lethal combination of disappointment, anger, and distrust. The fact that I had neither called nor come straight home after work was, in his eyes, unforgivable in a way not even a Sony PlayStation could ever make up for it.

At 4:00 a.m., when he had finally finished his *Friday the 13th* movie marathon and just before he went to sleep, he graciously woke me up to inform me that, if I ever wanted to restore peace in our home, the carpet had to go. By 6:30 a.m., after endless attempts to reclaim my sleep, I found myself clasping the carpet in the hallway outside our apartment. By 7:00 a.m., I began dragging myself and the carpet toward the subway station. I knew I would have to wait a few hours until the carpet shop opened, yet the thought of keeping the carpet within Ben's physical proximity and dealing with the circumstances was simply unbearable.

But the sun hadn't shined on me that day. Literally.

As I passed Mrs. Toda's temple gate, the sky suddenly went dark, and before I could move, massive amount of rain fell. I froze in place, feeling as if I was drowning both physically and emotionally.

"Sala-san?" I suddenly heard someone call out behind me. It was Mrs. Toda, who opened the gate to her temple and waved at me to come in for shelter.

I was surprised she even knew my name, but I still couldn't get myself to move. A few moments later, Mrs. Toda appeared, holding an umbrella over my head. There was nothing keeping me from entering her gate except the puddle of tears welling up in my eyes, which I knew would gush forth once I put the carpet down. But, with a wet carpet and a broken heart, I had nowhere else to go.

Mrs. Toda held the umbrella steadily above my head, despite my height, which was more than a head higher than hers, and led me to the entrance of the temple where she helped me remove my shoes and placed slippers on my feet. With my slippers on, she gestured with her hand for me to walk down the corridor with her. The corridor connected the temple with her living quarters and had a dark wooden floor. At its end, she slid open the door to a large, empty room. It was a traditional Japanese room with a tatami floor, which I assumed she kept for guests.

Standing at its entrance, looking into the open room, with a compassionate smile on her face, she said, "You can put your carpet here." Then she gently removed the carpet from my grip and began wiping the plastic underlay of the carpet with a small towel that she had grabbed from a nearby room. Once the carpet appeared dry, she helped me open it carefully, and we placed it on the tatami floor in the center of the room.

Although the actual situation seemed surreal and out of context, on one hand, it was as if she knew me and understood exactly what I was going through.

I sat down on the carpet and burst into tears. Mrs. Toda handed me a glass of water then retreated from the room with an approving, sympathetic smile.

Dharma, Mrs. Toda's white Persian cat, woke me up. At first, I had no idea where I was.

Dharma ran back and forth, poking at the carpet from all sides, suspiciously examining its passive nature. I sat up slowly and looked at him, amused by his energy and his unmet curiosity. Raising my eyes, I noticed Mrs. Toda standing in the doorway, equally entertained by Dharma. She asked no questions and, even more so, made me feel I had no need to explain.

As I collected myself and got up, she said in a quiet, motherly voice, "You can leave your carpet here."

Without giving it a second thought, I did. Just like that.

I put on the slippers that awaited me just beyond the door

of the room and followed Mrs. Toda down the wooden corridor and back to the temple area. As I walked behind her, I noticed just how tiny she was and how endearing, almost childish, her walk was. She swung her hands back and forth with every step, like a kid walking between both parents, cheerfully swinging her hands in theirs.

We bowed our heads slightly in respect then parted.

It was nearly 9:00 a.m., and only a tiny puddle of water at the entrance to our building reminded me of the rain that had caught me earlier. I walked into our home and found Ben still sound asleep. I lay down beside him and prayed that last night's episode would dissolve as the rain that was practically forgotten by the time I had left Mrs. Toda's temple. I wanted to go back to that simplicity we felt when we had just arrived. That feeling of two kids in the greatest playground ever.

I reached out for Ben's had, and he slowly opened it. Once he did, I could feel his strong, warm grip. My eyes watered, relieved to know he hadn't given up on me. I rested my other hand on his head, running my fingers gently through his hair.

"We'll get through this," I whispered to him, reminding myself how vulnerable and lonely he must have been feeling.

Ironically, and somewhat entertaining, what kept me most comforted that instant was the thought that my white carpet had found its place in the large, empty room with a white Persian cat and the singing widow of a Buddhist priest.

Chapter 8: Two Years After Moving To Tokyo

I was just about to insert my key in the keyhole of our front door when the delicious but overwhelming smell of French cooking hit my nostrils. *Beef bourguignon! Ben is home.* There was something so romantic about coming home to great smells of homemade cooking. However, Ben usually only went overboard when we had guests, and I couldn't recall inviting anyone for dinner, not when I was so badly jet-lagged.

"Hi, I'm home!" I called out from the entrance in my romantic-comedy voice, taking off my easy-to-slip-in-and-out-of, no heel—so I didn't look down at anyone—elegant yet fake Prada shoes.

From where I stood, I could see Ben sitting at our tiny kitchen bar, engrossed in the big recipe book that we had brought back from Provence last summer.

I put on my slippers and snuck up behind him, pressing my lips to the side of his neck gently, so as not to distract him.

"I invited the Levins over for dinner," he commented in a distant voice, still wrapped up in the recipe in front of him.

"Did we talk about having guests tonight?" I asked cautiously.

"No, but not everything has to work according to *your* schedule," he answered sharply, raising neither his voice nor his eyes.

It was clear to me that the dinner was a done deal, although I had just gotten back from a seventy-two-hour business trip, had slept only four hours, and had worked all day.

Ben rose from his seat and reached for the cupboard, pulling out a measuring cup.

I could understand Ben's need for company. After all, I traveled a lot. We used to have a larger group of friends, but many of them were now on Ben's blacklist. Just one small glitch or one wrong word considered inappropriate by Ben, and *whoops*, you were blacklisted.

Dan and Linda, my high school friends, had argued with me on my birthday about where we should all go out for dinner—*chaka-boom* blacklisted! My cousin Nora had happened to tell Ben that he had no sense of humor—*chaka-boom* blacklisted big time! In the case of the Satos, we had been invited to their home for dinner twice. Ben, being a great wine lover, had conscientiously selected wine for both occasions. The Satos, however, had chosen to serve beer instead. You guessed it. In short, the Levins were pretty much our only friends at that point.

I changed into the bathroom-only slippers, a custom Ben and I had adopted to make our Japanese friends more comfortable when visiting, and slid the door shut behind me.

Japanese toilets were the ideal showcase for ingenious

Japanese home appliance design with zero tolerance for wasted space. The toilets were small and functional, and they had a multitude of features for you to choose from, such as heated seats that made your winter visits more pleasant and soundtracks of natural running water to cover up any inhospitable sounds. The water tank for recycling purposes and space maximization converted into a small sink. You could rinse your hands with the same water that was then used for flushing the toilet.

Above the water tank hung a small mirror. I looked at my reflection and noticed how red my eyes were. I wondered if they were red because I was so desperately tired or because I wanted to burst into tears.

I walked past Ben and into the bedroom, closing the door behind me.

"What a mess!" I heard myself say out loud. I picked up my jacket then knelt down on the cold, wooden floor to collect the socks that had piled up under the chair beside our bed. Just then, the doorbell rang.

I forgot about the Levins!

"I need to change!" I called out to Ben just as he opened the front door.

Noah Levin worked for Microsoft Japan and had been living in Tokyo longer than any of our other non-Japanese acquaintances. In Japan, Western men were extremely popular, regardless of how geeky they were. So, from the moment he had arrived in Japan, even Noah, the ultimate nerd, had found himself constantly surrounded by sweet, giggly Japanese companions.

Then, one day, he had met Tomiko Tanaka, who had just

then relocated to Tokyo from the Kansai area of Japan. Recognizing Noah's need for a demanding woman who would resemble his constantly dissatisfied Jewish mother and determined they should marry, Tomiko had offered to convert to Judaism, knowing it would please his parents and thus encourage him to tie the knot. Now, chatty yet chic Tomiko Tanaka went by the name Rachel Levin. Her in-laws were delighted and proudly present her as their special prize at all public events.

By the time I joined them, they had all had a glass of wine and the mood seemed lively. As I took my seat, Noah turned toward me and asked how business was going.

Now, here is the thing, if you are looking to kill a conversation—and I was truly not in any fit state for getting into one—there is only one answer to this kind of question that will have the desired result …

"Business is great," I replied with my widest smile.

Silence.

Still smiling, I turned to Rachel and dropped the bomb, asking her about their recent holiday in Guam. Now that was a question with potential for a long-lasting answer, especially from Rachel.

As Rachel got going, the stage was set for the rest of the evening. She was more than happy to answer and embarked on her giggly monologue, while both men stared at her with attentive, adoring eyes.

Freedom!

I turned to my plate and tried to chew on the perfectly cooked meat. It was one of my favorite dishes yet, however much I wanted to enjoy it, nausea had taken over.

Ben turned his gaze my way just as I laid down the fork, still holding the small portion of juicy meat that I had keenly attempted to bite into. I could see how much Ben was awaiting my approval, as he did every time he got into a cooking craze, and I really didn't want to disappoint him, but I just could not bring the loaded fork to even touch my lips.

I looked down at my plate in despair then raised my eyes from my plate apologetically to find him still staring at me with that silent, passive-aggressive rage. It made no difference to him that my body was currently identifying with a time zone where beef was not its main priority. For Ben, it was part of my duty as his wife to reciprocate the efforts he had put into making the meal by enjoying it at any cost. *And* being expressive about it.

As soon as they had all finished eating, I silently cleared the table, and then we moved into the living room. I was two glasses of wine in and could hardly keep my eyes open. Rachel was still center stage, now reviewing the latest restaurants that she and Noah had visited …

The next thing I knew, I was in bed. I couldn't recall at what point I had fallen asleep. I didn't even have the slightest idea what time of day it was.

I rolled over and found Ben lying beside me. His eyes were wide open, facing my direction but looking right through me.

"When did I fall asleep?" I whispered softly to him.

Ben grabbed the edge of the blanket, covered his head, and then turned his back to me.

I searched for his hand, but he pushed me away. So, eventually, I turned over as well and looked out the window at the Tokyo Tower. I tried to close my eyes again, but I couldn't keep them shut. The smell of beef bourguignon still lingered in the air, and I lay in bed, wide awake, hungry yet nauseous.

Chapter 9: A Red Rose

Every evening, around 10:00 p.m., Tokyo subways had acquired a stench of alcohol, which miraculously faded away by the next morning. Tonight, to my great relief, I had managed to land a seat in the middle section. Sitting down was, without a doubt, the lesser evil compared to standing, squeezed in between drunken, overworked, sleepwalking Japanese men. My shoulder, however, was occupied by a grey-suited, white-collared drunk.

In a culture where physical contact between strangers was uncommon, this was not the first time a suited, intoxicated stranger had found comfort in crossing this subtle line and resting his head on my shoulder. To be honest, though, I was in no hurry to get home.

Last week, Ben had started writing another novel. He had already completed two; one was about an easygoing cowgirl who had lost her farm to a corrupt millionaire and had become a raging, revenge-seeking tax attorney, and the other was about a polygamous man with three sex-crazed wives. It began with a man on the verge of suicide after realizing that it was actually men who he desired. Anyway, both written novels had been rejected by all thirty-two agents who he had approached. I rather liked the concepts of both, but I had to admit that Ben's writing had a dark edge that could potentially turn off readers looking for light entertainment.

His current novel portrayed four individuals who each independently moved to Tokyo, their lives dramatically changing as a result. Ben had been interviewing people to get ideas for his characters, and Rachel Levin was apparently among his interviewees. Her life had definitely changed since moving to Tokyo and meeting Noah, since she had changed her name and had converted her religion together with her squid and eel eating habits.

In any case, when Ben was writing, the world around him must stand perfectly still, and so our life as a couple would turn into a slow, uneventful movie on mute. When Ben was conducting interviews, I was either exiled from our home or expected to maintain perfect silence while locked up in our bedroom in our very tiny accommodations. Lately, this routine had begun to make me feel more welcomed in my office than in my home. Add to that the silent treatment I had received following the whole beef bourguignon debacle last week ... and yes, my life was now a living hell.

Silent treatments were the worst! I wouldn't be surprised to discover it had first been initiated in response to the Ribbentrop-Molotov conspiracy as the Jewish's method of revenge. As torture went, I tried my best to resist, but sooner or later, I knew I would crack and begin apologizing, demonstrating all conceivable forms of regret. When my apologies were not met by humanitarian relief, I ended up in tears, begging Ben to stop, to simply say a word, to get it over with and out of his system and out of our way. There was usually some drama before the torture ended.

It took me years to realize how desperate I was at the end of the day for his approval. Although, seemingly, I did what I wanted. Things, however, were so much easier when Ben was happy or, at least, when he pretended to be or, at the very least, was vocal in some way or fashion.

"One more stop," I mumbled to myself.

It was nearly 11:00 p.m., and the zombie's head was still perched on my shoulder. *At least I am nearly home. It's time to start planning my exit strategy.* Well, to be precise, my train-exiting strategy.

I examined the most feasible path to the subway door and suddenly spotted Rachel Levin. It was odd to see her on our subway line at such a late hour, especially without Noah, her faithful guardian and companion.

As the subway came to a stop, Rachel and I were both washed out onto the platform with a wave of passengers. In an instant, Rachel disappeared in the crowd and, by the time I reached the station exit, she was nowhere to be seen.

I passed by the 7-Eleven, the pharmacy, and the small Buddhist temple where I had once left the white, fluffy carpet. Entering our apartment, I found a red rose on the kitchen bar. It had been a while since I had received anything even remotely romantic from Ben, so I was overcome with feelings that I hadn't felt toward him for a very long time.

I took a glass vase out of the cupboard and slipped the red rose into it. The rose stood tall and proud. Then I went into our bedroom and found Ben under the covers, peacefully sleeping. I kissed him gently on his forehead then removed my clothes before quietly molding myself around his fetal position. I inhaled the scent of his body and pushed closer to him, as if we were two rose petals.

As I lay there, unwinding from my very long day, the image of Rachel Levin on the subway interrupted my thoughts. Something about her being there tonight just didn't feel right.

Chapter 10: Unnoticed

A few weeks later, I woke up with the worst menstrual cramps. I didn't usually get them this bad.

I rolled out of bed, trying to put on a positive, productive smile while the center of my body rumbled like a volcano about to erupt. I grabbed the suit that I had worn a few days earlier, which was suspended from a hanger on the back of the bedroom door, sat on the edge of the bed, and slowly got dressed.

As I walked through the sliding glass doors and entered the office, I was astonished that I had actually survived the subway ride and endless underground passages leading from the station to our office building.

Mornings were always slow at the office, as if everyone sleepwalked their way to work, waking up only when safely parked in their cubicles. Some mornings, I was impatient with my colleagues, but today, I was actually relieved that I could take things slow. I just wanted this day to pass without anyone noticing me, especially my boss, Mr. Kobayashi.

Mr. Kobayashi practiced kendo, the art of Japanese swordsmanship. As a result, both his posture and his discipline were absolutely impeccable. Some would say he was the typical Japanese corporate boss. With a spine as stiff as a rod, he smiled very little and knew all the Japanese business rituals to a fault. He always looked neat and presentable—well, at least until he had a few drinks.

My first face-to-face encounter with Mr. Kobayashi had been on my way to the office on my first day at work. I had been heading toward the main building, passing through the parking lot, just as a Shinto priest was performing a purification ceremony on Mr. Kobayashi's new car. I had been quite amused that things like that actually happened in the center of Tokyo, at the beginning of the twenty-first century. Nonetheless, I loved the clash.

The priest had worn a tall, black hat, a white robe, and wide-legged, light-blue traditional pants. He had waved a wooden stick with strips of paper at its tip over the shiny new car, simultaneously chanting, bowing, and clapping his hands. Next to the priest had stood a deeply engaged man in a neat, grey suit. Throughout the ceremony, the man had waited perfectly still, an attentive expression on his face.

I had tried my best to walk by unnoticed, but I could sense my presence had not gone undetected. From the corner of my eye, I had seen the devotee slowly shifting his gaze in my direction.

Later that day, I had been called to my new boss's office. When I had realized that the devotee was, in fact, Mr. Kobayashi, my new boss, I had smiled apologetically and, in my most friendly voice, congratulated him on his new car.

"Thank you," he'd answered coldly, making it clear that personal issues were way off limits.

During my first months at the firm, Mr. Kobayashi's proper and detached attitude toward me had made me feel isolated. When assigned a task, he had expected me to deal with it on my own and had encouraged me not to approach him with questions. He had only tolerated mistakes as long as I could prove I had done my best. The most frustrating thing was that he had assigned me some of the same tasks over and over again.

Often, at night, I would wake up in a cold sweat, overcome by anxiety and tormented by the fact that I had brought Ben and myself all the way to Japan to do the same tasks I had done a million times before. Ben would wake up straight away and wrap me up in a blanket, like a wet puppy saved on a rainy day. Then he would hold me close to him and tell me that, if anyone could make it in Japan, it was me. Time after time, he had reassured me that we had made the choice of moving to Tokyo together, even though we both knew that, the next morning, as soon as I left and went to work, he would feel lost and resentful, and his depression would wake after hibernation and take over.

One day, I had decided to mention my frustration regarding Mr. Kobayashi's distanced and penalizing attitude toward me to Yuki, the guy who sat next to me in my cubicle. It had just been a few days after Yuki had opened up to me and had told me his unreal life story.

Basically, when Yuki had been a child, maybe five or six years old, his parents had taken him and his older brother to the local Shinto shrine to watch a children's sumo competition. They had thought it would be a nice family tradition, unaware of the impact it would have on Yuki. A few weeks later, Yuki's kindergarten teacher had approached his parents, complaining that Yuki had been "sumo wrestling" with kids during the lunch breaks, landing quite a few of them in the dirt.

Deeply ashamed, Yuki's parents had asked him to fix his improper behavior, but Yuki wouldn't stop wrestling. Eventually, his helpless and disgraced parents had decided to take him back to the shrine and consult with the Shinto priest. Unexpectedly, the priest had advised them to let Yuki actually train in sumo and pursue that path. They had soon discovered Yuki's exceptional skills for this respectable, albeit body-deforming, Japanese art, and it had become clear that sumo was a part of their son's destiny.

To fulfill this predetermined life path, they had begun feeding him three times the amount of food consumed by his older brother and had escorted him to sumo competitions the length and breadth of Japan's four main islands. By the time Yuki had turned fifteen, he'd been a sumo star. There had been great expectations of him until, one day, Yuki had seen a TV documentary and understood that his life expectancy would be twenty years less than his average compatriot.

With the same discipline and determination that he had used to win his toughest matches, Yuki had lost nearly one hundred and twenty-six pounds in less than two years. Today, he was, without a doubt, the best-looking Japanese man I'd ever met—flamboyantly gay, who dressed to kill. He still loved watching sumo matches and, oddly or not, the immense proportions of sumo wrestlers seemed to reflect his current choice in men.

So, naturally, my more subtle confession to Yuki

regarding my frustration with Mr. Kobayashi's attitude toward me was nothing our relationship could not handle.

Surprisingly, Yuki had explained that Mr. Kobayashi was simply training me to always do my very best. He'd added that Mr. Kobayashi's dissatisfaction was a sign that he cared and felt that I was worth the trouble and not the contrary. Since that day, not only had my sense of self-worth been restored, but I had also gained Yuki as a truly trusted friend.

A few hours into the day, the menstrual pain became so overpowering that I could no longer hide it. On my way back from the kitchenette to my cubicle, Yuki stood from his seat and gently removed the glass of water from my unstable hand.

"You look as if you've seen a ghost," Yuki whispered to me, and I realized I was busted.

With a great deal of discomfort, I collected my belongings and excused myself, surrendering to my first ever menstrual day off work, a common custom for women working in Japan.

As I walked through the endless underground tunnels of my office subway station, I was absolutely drained, as if every ounce of life had been sucked out of me. I stopped at a vending machine and bought a can of hot English tea (yes, in Japan, they sell hot drinks in cans, as well! Brilliant, I know!).

The ride home was relatively fast, and seeing Tokyo at midday filled me with nostalgia for the days when I had still been a tourist with a dream. I reached my station and dragged myself onto the platform toward the escalator. *Whoever invented the escalator should have received a Nobel Peace Prize*, I thought to myself.

I suddenly remembered reading about some German-

Jewish guy who, before the war, had owned a department store somewhere in Germany, which was the first department store with an escalator. He had escaped to the U.S. during the war. But, as I tried to remember where I had read that, I suddenly noticed Rachel Levin walking about nine or ten steps ahead of me. This time, I was almost sure we had made actual eye contact, but when I reached ground level, she was gone. I couldn't figure out why she hadn't stopped and waited for me to catch up, or at least said hi. And I was quite sure she had seen me.

I headed out toward the station exit then paced in the direction of home.

Just as I was about to pass the Buddhist temple, I heard a commotion from the other side of Mrs. Toda's gate. I couldn't stop myself and soon was peeking in from over the gate to make sure that Mrs. Toda was okay.

She was on the temple deck, and a delicate-looking woman stood beside her. Two little girls, who I assumed belonged to the young woman, were running around the garden, yelling, "Dharma! Dharma!" in their high-pitched voices.

Mrs. Toda had a troubled expression on her face, her mushroom-style haircut, always neat, was a mess, and her eyes were darting in all directions. Although I felt deep sympathy for her, she seemed to be in good hands and, in my physical state, I couldn't see how I could be any help to her.

I turned back from the gate, ready to continue home, when deep, masculine laughter caught my attention. I looked back and, beyond the gate, was a well-built man with rolled-up sleeves, gently carrying Dharma, Mrs. Toda's cat. The white ball of fur seemed relaxed and self-assured in his manly hands, and the two little girls ran toward them in excitement.

I turned away from the gate again, ready to continue back home, just when Mrs. Toda noticed me.

"Sala-san," she called out cheerfully.

So much for leaving without being noticed, I said to myself, smiling at her as I opened the temple gate. I trudged along the immaculate path in the direction of Mrs. Toda when I suddenly fell to my knees, weakened, and the tiny pebbles at my feet seemed ...

I regained consciousness and found myself lying on my white, furry ex-carpet. Mrs. Toda was sitting above me, softly wiping my forehead with a cold, damp towel. When she noticed my eyes open, she swiveled elegantly on her knees and fixed me a bowl of green tea, stirring the green powder skillfully with a bamboo utensil.

I stared at her as she carefully lifted my head and served me the thick, bitter, green liquid. A few minutes later, I found the strength to carefully lift myself up and saw Dharma sitting beside her, also staring at me with compassionate eyes.

When I felt ready, Mrs. Toda accompanied me to the gate, waving at me until I vanished inside my building. It was nearly 4:00 p.m., and I was relieved to finally be home, as if it had been days since I had left the office.

I put on my slippers and lurched toward the sofa. As I walked into the living room, the window facing the main street was open, and I heard a deafening noise.

We never open that window.

Getting closer, I saw white sheets of paper scattered across the living room floor.

Ben used two types of paper to write his novels: yellow and white. The yellow paper was for his private notes, including interviews, recollections of dreams, and random thoughts. These were strictly private. His manuscript drafts were occasionally shown to others for review, and these were always on white sheets.

Why would Ben's manuscript be scattered around the room like that? I asked myself, shutting the window.

Finally, there was silence.

I called out to Ben, but he didn't answer.

I felt my knees buckling once more and pulled myself to the sofa. A million scenarios ran through my mind.

I then forced myself up and headed to the kitchen for a glass of water. That was when I noticed Ben's hand on the floor, sticking out from behind the kitchen bar. Barely able to breathe, I got down on my knees and crawled toward him, not knowing what to expect.

Ben was lying there, perfectly still.

I came closer and, as I ran my hand over his cheek, I noticed a tear making its way from the corner of his eye and down to my finger. I could feel the blood run through my veins again.

"Are you okay?" I asked.

Ben remained silent, as if all his words had been blown away with his notes. However, he nodded just enough for me to know he was conscious.

During his writing periods, such episodes occurred once in a while. He would have a fit then go numb. I had learned to deal with them somehow, but I always missed a heartbeat when they occurred. I had urged him a few times to meet with a psychiatrist during our visits to the States, and each time I mentioned it, he resented me for it, then followed the silent treatment, so I'd basically given up.

I leaned back on the kitchen cabinets, closing my eyes.

When I awoke, I found that I had passed out once more. Ben was, however, back at his laptop on the kitchen bar.

"Hey!" I called out to him.

"Hey," he answered from behind the screen, his eyes fully engaged on what he was doing, consumed in his own reality.

I stared at him in disbelief. *He scares the living daylights out of me then leaves me passed out on the kitchen floor?*

He then got up and, for a moment, I thought he was actually coming to lend me a hand, but he turned the other way and came back a few moments later with his yellow notes.

I tried to overlook this insignificant behavior on his end and took his pause from the screen as an opportunity to try to tell him about my day. I started with telling him how bad I'd felt at work, and that I was so pale that Yuki had urged me to go home. He didn't show much interest.

Then I mentioned how I had passed out on the pebble path at Mrs. Toda's temple, hoping that would appear significant enough for him to react. I could see he heard me, but it was clear he wasn't really listening.

I got up and called it a day.

Chapter 11: The Japanese Spirit

Japanese curry with the boys, or soba noodles with the girls? That was pretty much my daily dilemma around this hour when hunger started showing its signs. Personally, I'd do curry every day of the week, but Yuki always urged me to try to bond with my female colleagues. Sometimes, I thought he just wanted the boys all to himself.

"Curry is not considered very ladylike in Japan," Yuki reminded me often, and on certain days, I fell for this lame excuse.

But curry or not, I didn't think I'd ever be as "ladylike" as any of the Japanese women in our office, with their petite figures, million-dollar Gucci skirts, and impossibly high heels.

I rummaged for my employee badge under a ton of papers that had magically piled up on my desk since this morning and reached for my fake Prada purse at the bottom of my knockoff Louis Vuitton bag.

Just as I was about to go stalk my male colleagues for the curry lunch option, Mr. Kobayashi showed up at my cubicle with an all too familiar nervous look on his face.

"Sala-san! Mr. Inui is on his way to our office right now," he notified me then continued toward the meeting room as if the fire alarm had just gone off and the conference room was the designated gathering area.

For the past three years, we had been working on a merger between the automotive company that Mr. Inui worked for and a major European automotive company. Communication between the heads of the negotiating teams hadn't been smooth, to say the least. Neither Mr. Inui, who I code-named the "Sweaty Swine," nor his European counterpart were easy people to deal with.

My secret code-name for the head of the European negotiation team was the "Silky-Haired Tap Dancer in Disguise," since he had shown up for dinner every night this week with what looked like tap dancing shoes, as if planning to sneak off after dinner to the International Tap Dancers Reunion, if there even was such a thing.

We'd just concluded four intensive, productive days of meetings, and the Europeans were due to leave tonight, which explained Mr. Kobayashi's concern for an unscheduled meeting today. The Japanese party seldom initiated spontaneous meetings, and when they did, it was never a good sign. We'd prepared quite a few financial scenarios by now, and our analyses all showed that this merger had great potential for both parties.

Obediently, I shoved my purse back into my bag then quickly followed Mr. Kobayashi across our floor and into the meeting room.

Mr. Inui and his team arrived before the Europeans. His team included three young men; two of whom looked younger than me. In Japan, you never really knew. There was a serious air to their expressionless presence.

I sat across from one of the younger men, surveying the half-empty room that would soon fill with even more tension, and I was suddenly aware of how stiff my neck was.

Ben's mood swings had been very drastic lately, and he had taken to throwing drafts of his manuscript out the window, an odd pattern that had started the day I had left work early with menstrual pain.

His parents had arrived this morning, just after I had left for work. They were staying with us for a week then traveling to Korea for a weekend on their way back home. They had bought cheap last-minute tickets and had thought it would be nice to surprise us. This had topped all of their glorified denials. Well, I was no less in denial, I guess, or perhaps desperately hopeful that, although Ben hated surprises, this would actually be able to cheer him up. Instead, ever since they had notified us of their plans, Ben had been more anxious and difficult than usual.

Yesterday had probably been his worst day. When I had gotten home from work, I had found him sitting in the corner of our living room, on the floor, staring at the wall. It'd been clear he had been crying, possibly for hours.

After failing to get a single word out of him for what seemed like eternity, he had finally caved and looked in my direction. I'd sat there, hugging him until his body slowly surrendered like a sinking battleship. Then I had helped support him as we walked to the bedroom where, wrapped in my arms, he'd descended into a deep, blue sleep.

Ben had unresolved issues with his parents, especially

with his father. His father was a retired Navy officer who had had a well-respected career with all types of awards and honors. Ben claimed his father was his ultimate childhood hero, but ever since I'd known Ben, he always seemed disappointed and even somewhat ashamed of his father. It was true that, since he had retired, his father did very little, simply worked in the garden, read books, and hosted BBQs for his old Navy friends, which sometimes ended with a tad more alcohol in his blood than could be expected from a decent man his age. But I saw nothing wrong with his lifestyle.

My stomach yelled, *hunger!* bringing my consciousness back to the meeting room. I sat still for a moment, wondering whether everyone had heard my stomach or just me. I pulled my chair closer to the table, hoping to cover up any future protests from within. Then I did my best to try to figure out what I'd missed while my mind had drifted off.

My boss seemed to be trying some Japanese schmoozing, while the OL was quietly serving green tea. It was obvious that Mr. Inui, the "Sweaty Swine," was ready to fire and was simply waiting for the OL to leave.

"I am troubled by the future merger of the electric car unit," he stated firmly as the door closed behind the OL, sweat starting to light up his forehead.

From the very start, Mr. Inui had been very particular, even slightly emotional, about the electric car unit, perhaps because he was part of one of the first teams globally to initiate the concept.

"Ooo ... I hate it when that happens!" I suddenly snapped as my stomach again yelled, *hunger!*

The room grew silent. Everyone sat up in their seats,

offering me their full attention. I understood that they, not surprisingly, thought that my sudden "Ooo" had something to do with the conversation that Mr. Inui and Mr. Kobayashi were having. Their silence assured me that it wasn't going anywhere until I played my part.

Accepting my fate and embracing the fact that I seemed to have no choice, I took my best shot.

"The Europeans just don't get the Japanese spirit!" I hoped I sounded relevant and somehow convincing, but more than anything, I tried to show empathy to Mr. Inui's distress.

I could see by the anxious expression on Mr. Kobayashi's face that it might not have been the best choice of words. Mr. Inui, on the other hand, looked intrigued by my sudden outburst and stared at me, anticipating more.

I had no idea what to say, so I turned to my cup of green tea, picked it up in my right hand, and put my left hand at the bottom, trying to appear as graceful as my Japanese women friends, while buying time. With a mindful expression, I took a dainty sip of tea, slowly set the cup down on the table in front of me, and then raised my eyes, looking back at Mr. Inui with the most unpretentious expression I could manage.

No one has moved an inch. My tea-sipping pause seemed only natural to the Japanese, who were never in a hurry to say anything.

I could feel my hands begin to sweat and, just as I opened my mouth to continue, the Silky-Haired Tap Dancer in Disguise entered the room with his team.

I never thought I would be so happy to see him, I said to myself, both amused and relieved.

My eyes drifted toward his feet as they had every day

since I had first seen him with his tap shoes. The funny thing was that, somehow, even with the slippers that he had received from reception, he still had that tap dancer's walk, only now it was muted. I always found it entertaining that, no matter how well you dressed for a meeting in Japan, as soon as you reached your client's office, you were forced into those ugly, one-size-fits-all slippers.

I got up to greet him and his team but, more importantly, to accompany him to his designated seat.

The OL came in again. This time, she offered a more diverse variety of beverages.

I took advantage of the short intermission to sneak a peek at my vibrating cell phone, finding a text message from Ben.

Rachel & Noah will join us on Sat.

I was relieved. Going sightseeing alone with Ben's parents was no walk in the park. Ben's mother loved window shopping, just without the windows, and stopped at every single store, touched every single item on every single shelf, bought nothing, and drove us all crazy, especially Ben's father. He, on the other hand, revived his Navy officer habits and planned our days from morning until night, setting a rigid timetable and constantly notifying us on how long we had left before our "next assignment."

The best thing about Rachel and Noah joining us was that, in the presence of strangers and, all the more so, locals, Ben's parents tended to act a bit more like normal people. They were somewhat pleasant, relatively cooperative and, in some instances, could be mistaken for the perfect, easygoing travelers. In short, there was a good chance we would survive the weekend.

For some reason, the meeting took on a better tone than had been expected. Mr. Inui seemed to have released some of the tension that he had arrived with before the Europeans had gotten there. The action item was for both parties to present their branding concepts for the electric car unit at the next meeting.

I got up when signaled to and, while I walked the European team to reception, I considered the fastest way to pacify my raging hunger once I was finally excused.

The elevator shut and, the Europeans beyond my jurisdiction, I returned to the meeting room and quietly sat, praying to the hunger god that we were close to the end.

Mr. Inui, who was talking with Mr. Kobayashi, suddenly stopped mid-sentence. As he turned my way, I looked at him apologetically, hoping I hadn't interrupted his line of thought.

"Sala-san, we will close the deal when you have explained to our European friends what the Japanese spirit is," he said, his smile exposing his dark, ununified front teeth, which reminded me of the remains of a cracked lobster.

I thought it was the first time I'd ever seen him smile, and although it was a relief, I concluded the sight of his lips scrunched together in anger, despite the sweat, might have been easier to glance at.

Mr. Kobayashi smiled at me sympathetically, and there was no way back.

"I will do my best," I answered, having no other choice. Then I smiled back hesitantly.

I left the office at 6:00 p.m., the earliest I'd left this year. Well, except for the day of the menstrual pain. There was still some daylight outside, and the drunken zombies hadn't yet hit the rails.

My guilt quickly transformed into an elevated sense of freedom. On the way home from the station, I stopped at the 7-Eleven and bought some Japanese-style TV dinners. I grabbed a dish of Japanese curry, as well, though it didn't seem as appetizing as the curry I would have eaten at lunch with the boys.

I passed the pharmacy and the temple. It was karaoke night, and the lights were out in Mrs. Toda's residence. I headed up the street and reached my building. Approaching my apartment, I took a deep breath, counted to three, and then walked in.

"I'm home!" I called out cheerfully to Ben as I changed into slippers.

Ben showed up in an instant, whispering and hushing me with panic in his eyes. "Careful, don't wake them! They are finally asleep!"

"Sorry," I whispered. "I brought dinner," I added, handing over the plastic bags.

Ben quietly took the trays out of the bags and heated them up in the microwave while I changed out of my suit and into my cozy pajamas.

We sat down at the kitchen bar, and then Ben turned to me and said, "I am sorry about last night. I don't know how you put up with me." He looked down at his food, his eyes filling with tears.

"You are my husband," I answered. "The most important investment of my life," I added, quoting another of my father's mottos.

A tear made its way down Ben's cheek, and I could see

how delicate and fragile he was.

"I don't know how *you* tolerate *me*!" I said, a mock-serious expression on my face. "What kind of wife am I? I show off at work, bragging that I am going home early to cook dinner for you and my parents-in-law, and then I come home with ready-made food from 7-Eleven!"

Ben managed a reserved smile and wiped the tears from his cheeks.

We broke apart our disposable chopsticks and reached for the trays. I was so hungry that the food from 7-Eleven tasted like manna from heaven. After a few gratifying bites, my mind went blank. I forgot about Ben's moods, his deep-sleeping, high-maintenance parents, and my promise to Mr. Inui regarding the Europeans and the Japanese spirit.

Chapter 12: Couples

There has always been many myths about in-laws, and especially about the mother- and daughter-in-law relationship. In my case, they were all true. In Mrs. Rosenberg's eyes, I was born to serve her and worship her son. It wasn't that I didn't do my best to make Ben happy. Still, she found interesting ways to point out to me the importance of being obedient and pleasing my husband. This morning was a classic example.

Ben refused to accept my physical and emotional need to wear sneakers when going sightseeing. For me, it was part of the deal. If we were taking the day off to enjoy ourselves, so should my feet. It might have to do with him being raised by a mother who was always elegantly attired from head to toe. She made wearing high heels seem so natural that one could easily picture her mountain climbing, diving with great white sharks, and skiing down Everest, all in her stylish, pointy heels. And so, if even the thought of sneaking into my sneakers crossed my mind, I was doomed! *I wonder if that is why they call them sneakers ...*

As soon as Ben noticed me reaching for them, he muttered unreservedly, "So, you want to look like the cleaning lady?" Then he went one step further and shot me one of *those* looks.

His customary reaction to the issue pretty much killed off any spark of enthusiasm for the day. Disappointed, I chose some less comfortable yet more elegant alternative, hoping the physical pain would be more manageable this time.

So, after that footwear incident, as the four of us headed out to the station, Ben's mother slowed her pace to meet mine, turned to me, and said, "You did the right thing. You should be grateful my son cares about what you wear. Isn't it important to you? You do want to make Ben happy, don't you?"

Ooo ... I hate it when she does this! I found myself yelling inside my head as I forced my hands into the pockets of my tight blue jeans so that I didn't pull my hair out in rage.

If she only knew how much I try to make Ben happy ...

Then I reminded myself that I'd been through this scene a million times before, and that there was no point trying to answer her back, as I would eventually surrender. And so, I turned on my very best smile and kept it in place for ten seconds straight.

Registering my smile, she smiled back, satisfied, and my mission was accomplished. *Bingo!* I was the master of all mothers-in-law. The avalanche had been averted.

We continued toward the station, both looking down at our fancy shoes as we quietly walked behind our men. Grateful for her silence, my cheeks gradually cooled down. And as my eyes shifted from my shoes to hers, I was suddenly struck by a revelation. *Is it possible that Mrs. Rosenberg is suffering just as much in her heels? Could it be that she endures the pain only because she believes it makes Mr. Rosenberg happy?* The possibility that I might be right and that our suffering was mutual instantaneously improved my mood.

The four of us took the subway two stops north, where we met up with Noah and Rachel. We had decided to start the day in Kamakura, one of Japan's historical capitals, about an hour out of Tokyo. Kamakura was a well-known tourist destination, due to its famous Buddhist temple, toting a forty-two-foot-tall seated Buddha known as the Daibutsu.

On arriving in Kamakura, we made straight for the Daibutsu. We entered the temple and, predictably, Ben's mother rapidly found her way to the gift shop. Ben's father hurried after her, and Ben followed them both to make sure they didn't kill each other on the temple's sacred grounds. On the Levin front, Noah accompanied Rachel to the washroom so that she could literally powder her nose, and I found myself standing alone at the feet of the massive, sanctified statue.

I stared intently at the Daibutsu, trying to draw out some spiritual vibe, and although it wasn't my first visit, it was the first time that I really examined the Buddha's magnitude. Its remarkable dimensions led me to a thought far from spiritual and utterly out of context.

God as my witness, I literally had no idea why, of all possible thoughts, this one took over: *Does size really matter?*

As the thought and very odd images echoed through my mind, I muttered to myself in shame, *You are in a temple, staring at a Buddha, for heaven's sake!* But I simply could not switch off my internal dialogue.

What if he can actually hear my thoughts?

I battled the voice in my head, put on a devoted expression, and tried to allow the Buddha's supreme serenity to penetrate me.

Okay, forget the word "penetrate."

"You are Sala-san, right?" My line of thought was suddenly interrupted by a deep voice. No, it wasn't the Buddha; it was the voice of the man standing next to me.

I nodded in affirmation then turned toward him, realizing he looked familiar. I examined him quizzically, but I just couldn't work out where I knew him from.

"Do you need an explanation, or are you familiar with the Daibutsu?" he continued confidently.

I transferred my gaze to the Buddha then looked back at the man. *I know those hands*, I thought to myself, staring at him with a baffled smile on my face. I then spotted two little girls behind him, and it registered. *They were the ones helping Mrs. Toda when Dharma went missing a few months ago.*

"I usually get to know a woman before she passes out in my arms," he added without warning, as if reading my mind and realizing I had just now figured out how we had met, a charming smile on his face.

I ran all possible scenarios through my mind until I realized it made perfect sense. The man with the rolled-up sleeves must have been the one who had carried me from the pebble path to the guest room at Mrs. Toda's residence.

I blushed and felt an awkward smile take over.

"Did I interrupt you in the middle of a prayer or meditation?" he continued.

"No," I quickly replied. "I was just thinking of the Daibutsu and how enormous it is." My eyes dropped to the ground where I couldn't help but notice how large my companion's feet were.

What the hell is wrong with me?

Fortunately, the pretty woman from Mrs. Toda's temple showed up with the two little girls, and the provocative images in my head instantly evaporated. The four of them smiled at me politely.

Then the man with the large hands and even larger feet leaned toward me and said in a soft yet suggestive voice, "I hope to see you again … Sala-san." He lifted the two girls, one in each arm, and then they cheerfully waved goodbye.

I took a deep breath as Rachel and Noah returned from what seemed like a very long "nose powder." The three of us took a moment to observe the great statue then wandered over to the gift shop to retrieve the Rosenbergs.

The two men stood side by side, arms folded, wearing identical expressions, while waiting impatiently for Mrs. Rosenberg, who was debating which postcard to buy.

We eventually left the temple and strolled through the ancient capital, enjoying the good weather and the first signs of autumn. Next on our schedule was Meiji Shrine in Tokyo.

A good balance of Shinto and Buddhism in one day never hurt the sense of accomplishment of the single-minded tourist.

We walked to the station. The platform was packed, as to be expected on a Saturday. Taking our place in line, I was astonished once again by just how polite and positive the Rosenbergs were around Noah and Rachel.

So far so good! I thought to myself.

We arrived at Meiji Shrine, walked through the gate leading to the shrine, and just happened to chance upon a young Japanese couple on their way to their wedding ceremony. The bride and groom, in their traditional dress, looked magical, as if they had just escaped from the set of a samurai movie. They paraded through the shrine grounds with their heavy, uncomfortable-looking yet perfect outfits, the bride emitting a sense of sheer elegance under an extraordinary hairstyle. They radiated an almost sacred ceremonial essence.

On their feet and carrying the excessive weight of their costumes, they wore *geta*—elevated Japanese traditional wooden flip-flops, which could honestly be used as objects of torture.

I stared at the couple smoothly gliding by in their *geta*, postures upright, as if walking on air.

"Are you coming?" Ben asked impatiently. "Sarah?"

I could hear him, but my eyes found it difficult to disengage from the perfection they were witnessing.

"Hello! Anyone there?" Ben finally raised his voice.

I slowly shifted my eyes toward Ben and smiled as he grabbed my hand and pulled me along. A few moments later, I looked back and realized the bride and groom were gone.

Ben was still holding my hand, but his grip was strong, and there was nothing slightly romantic about it. We walked through Meiji Shrine, I following his lead, as he threw a few coins in the offering box then clapped his hands to catch the attention of the spirits, as the ritual required. We then strolled to the imperial gardens.

I detached myself from Ben, slowed my pace, and tried to enjoy the gardens. They were beautiful at all times of the year and were a perfect getaway from the intensity of Tokyo.

It seemed like they were also a great way to keep Mrs. Rosenberg far away from the shops, thus keeping Mr. Rosenberg's blood pressure in check.

We ended the day at an okonomiyaki restaurant. The concept was that the diners received a hotplate and ingredients, and then each diner created their own meal. First, you spread a layer of ready-made batter on the hotplate, and then you chose from a variety of toppings. My Japanese friends referred to okonomiyaki as a Japanese-style pizza, but I thought it was more like a savory pancake. The best thing about this choice of dining with the Rosenbergs was that we were spared Mrs. Rosenberg's chatter as she was too preoccupied with touching all the different sauce bottles and toppings laid out on the table in front of us.

I personally didn't find okonomiyaki so tasty, but it was definitely something that foreigners wrote home about. What I did like about okonomiyaki was that it always reminded me of my year in Hiroshima, as Hiroshima was famous for its okonomiyaki. Japanese people were more likely to ask me how I found the okonomiyaki in Hiroshima than how I found living in one of the two cities in the world ever to be hit by an atomic bomb. To me, that was the essence of how the Japanese wanted to see the world—as long as you could keep things more positive than negative, then you were doing well in a culture that was constantly creating the future.

Chapter 13: Lost In Japan

As soon as the Rosenbergs left, things at home started getting back to normal—well, better than our normal, actually. Some days, Ben and I even enjoyed a fun evening out together. His moods were still as unpredictable as snow in springtime, but all in all, it seemed as though we had learned to contain the swings.

At work, however, the pressure was on. Over the span of five weeks, I ended up traveling to Europe three times to meet with the European automotive team. I was first sent there to identify possible gaps between the visions of both parties and to try to minimize those gaps as much as possible before the two teams met again. I cross-examined the Europeans dozens of times and gathered all the information I could think of. Nevertheless, each time I reported back to Mr. Kobayashi, he would send me back with a new list of questions, as if I had done no research at all. Again, the same pattern as before. That, too, I learned to contain. Working for a Japanese firm was the career choice I had made, and this was simply the way business was done here.

My last trip to Europe had been cut short by a day due to

a personal matter concerning the Silky-Haired Tap Dancer in Disguise. The truth was that I was emotionally ready to go back to Japan and felt quite confident that I might finally meet Mr. Kobayashi's expectations.

I was able to get a flight out a day earlier than originally planned, and when I arrived at the check-in counter, I upgraded to business class, which convinced me that my early return was meant to be.

The business-class section of the aircraft was more spacious than I recalled from the last time I had peeked through the dividing curtains. I took my single digit seat, put my feet up, and let the chair massage my back. I planned my entertainment schedule, zipping through the channels on my personal screen. When the duty-free items were brought around, I decided to use up all my loose euros and buy Ben their finest bottle of whiskey and most exclusive chocolates. I felt as if I'd been given a glimpse into the lives of top executives and, just for a moment, I fantasized that someone was watching me, wondering which Fortune 500 company I led.

I opened the in-flight travel magazine to the page displaying photos of first-class honeymoon suites in Bora-Bora then tucked the open magazine into the seat pocket in front of me, just enough for the mesmerizing snapshots to show. I ordered the most elaborate meal on the menu, trying to reproduce a slight French accent, although I hadn't the vaguest idea what I was actually ordering.

I asked for champagne with and between every single meal, as if it were my daily tipple, but unfortunately, the champagne gag was what seemed to blow my cover. By the time we were in the middle of nowhere, above no-man's land, I was throwing up so violently that all I could remember was yelling out, in-between waves of nausea, "Nothing good ever came from the French!"

An hour before we landed, I finally fell asleep. Twenty minutes later, the flight attendant woke me and asked me to lift the back of my seat for landing.

Poof! The last of my perks, the reclining seat, taken away ... just like that! I was left to land, shuffling in my seat, just like the simple people of economy class.

I passed out on the train ride home, and when I opened my eyes, it took me a moment to realize where I was. The local time was only 10:00 a.m., and the fact that I had a whole day ahead of me to recover before going back to work cheered me up, especially since I hadn't received an SOS call from Ben during the trip, thus I was optimistic he might actually be in a good mood.

I got off the train and took my regular route home. Everything around me seemed peaceful and relaxed—yet another sign this could be a great day. I passed the 7-Eleven where three young men were standing around, reading manga books above the magazine shelves. I was relieved to be back in Japan.

At the pharmacy, Akiko smiled pleasantly at the customers, as if there were no illnesses in the world. Mrs. Toda was sweeping her path industriously, while Dharma watched from the temple deck with admiration. There was a smell of autumn in the air, and the leaves had dramatically changed their colors since I'd left. It was that time of year, just before the cold winter set in, when romance was in the air.

I suddenly missed Ben and quickened my pace, anxious to get home.

I took off my shoes at the entrance and quietly snuck in. I hoped Ben would find my early return a pleasant surprise, despite the fact that he wasn't a surprise type of guy. Perhaps we would spend a romantic day together or just enjoy a lazy day in bed. We used to love those lazy days in bed when we had just met, but that seemed so long ago now.

I walked through the kitchen, dining room, and living room. I even peeked into the bathroom and toilet, but I didn't see Ben. *He must still be sleeping*, I thought to myself, softly opening the bedroom door. The bed was empty. I was rather disappointed, but then I recalled that it was probably for the best. I was, after all, a post-champagne, vomiting machine on the loose, and for humanitarian reasons, sparing him the pleasure of my company and stench might, in fact, be the truest act of love.

I stepped into the bath to take a shower, showerhead in hand with steaming water cascading over my head. I felt myself returning from the dead—i.e. vomiting hell. I shampooed twice, trying to revive my hair. I then scrub myself thoroughly, as the Japanese had taught me. And when I said thoroughly, I really meant thoroughly … everywhere. I was not proud to admit that only at the age of twenty-five, when living in Hiroshima, had I learned to scrub myself everywhere for the first time.

This might sound a bit strange, but I had been exposed to this eye-opening experience only when Noriko-chan had come to collect me one evening at my employee housing to go together to the local public bath. When she had arrived, I had grabbed a plastic basket, threw in a bottle of shampoo, conditioner, and soap, hung a towel over my shoulder, and had been ready to go. She had looked into my basket and, with a big question mark on her face, had asked, "How are you planning to scrub the middle of your back?" She had then reached into her basket and pulled out an extra back scrubbing cloth for me. Until that day, the thought of scrubbing the middle of my back had never even crossed my mind nor, as far as I knew, had it crossed the minds of at least two thirds of humanity.

Okay, I am still standing in the shower. I must have been daydreaming. The water was pounding me like a mid-summer monsoon, and I never wanted it to end. I couldn't recall when I last felt so comforted and spoiled, and I realized that I truly thirsted for some nurturing.

I closed my eyes and felt the warmth of the water spread to every inch of my body. I felt as if I could spend all the remaining hours of the day in my wet paradise.

Then, all of a sudden, dizziness consumed me. I leaned back against the wall and opened my eyes in a slight panic. My energy was gone all at once, and all I wanted to do was sleep.

I quickly turned off the shower and reached for the towel. My arm was a dead weight. Exhaustion took over, and I carefully exited the shower. I hardly dried myself off, to be honest. I only hoped to make it to the bedroom.

I wondered if it was the jet lag, a hangover, or pure exhaustion after weeks of long work days that had finally taken their toll.

At a certain point, I woke up to find myself lying on top

of the blanket, my towel wrapped around me. I couldn't remember when or how I had gotten there. My hair was still damp, and I was just about capable of covering myself with the blanket. I fell back into a deep sleep.

Once again, I woke up disoriented. Seeing Tokyo Tower through the window, I realized I was home. Judging from the light outside, it looked as if it was late afternoon, maybe early evening. All I wanted to do was sleep. I wondered where Ben was but couldn't even bring myself to fetch my cell phone from the kitchen bar to call him.

I dozed in and out of sleep and, at some point, I felt as if I'd been poisoned or drugged. I was terribly thirsty. It was a very scary feeling. I wanted to wake up but could not bring myself around.

I tried calling out to Ben, wondering if he was home yet, but I simply could not produce a sound. I wasn't sure if I was dreaming or awake.

I heard an odd word here and there that made me feel even more lost.

"I never meant to … I can leave if you want."

I surrendered and fell back into a deep sleep.

I found myself still lying in bed, staring once again at Tokyo Tower. Surrounded by the colors of sunrise, the city looked as peaceful as it did walking back home from the station yesterday. I rolled over, surprised to find Ben lying beside me. I was relieved to see him.

I moved myself closer to him, trying to get his attention, like an eager puppy. I was so thirsty that I would do anything for a sip of water. I was still weak yet bringing myself closer to him so that I could ask him for some water. Then I noticed that he was fully dressed, hands folded on his chest, eyes fixed on the ceiling. He was actually awake.

I tried to whisper out to him, but I couldn't.

"Hi," I finally mumbled softly, trying to make my embrace more obvious, while my body recovered from its long rest.

There was silence.

I tried to figure out his expression and finally noticed how his lips were pursed in a serious mode. I wasn't sure why Ben wasn't answering and why there was tension in the air.

I brushed my fingers lightly through his hair, and he pushed my hand away.

"Did you hear a word of what I've been saying?" he shot at me irritably.

I was stunned by his hostility, and it took me a few moments before it all came rushing back to me. The words that were scattered in my mind started to piece together slowly in faint, unwelcome phrases. Although I was emotionally all over the place, and physically in distress, suddenly everything was perfectly clear. I had not been dreaming nor hallucinating. The words I had heard had been real.

A very dark feeling took over, as if my world was coming to an end and the sun itself had betrayed me by choosing never to rise again. I wanted to stop the noise building up in my head. I sat in bed, carefully and attentively looking at Ben.

The only words to come out of my mouth were, "I am not sure I understand."

"What do you need to understand?" he replied, still agitated and still staring at the ceiling.

"Water. Could you bring me some water?" I suddenly

said, realizing I couldn't think straight until I was even slightly rejuvenated.

He handed me a half-filled glass of water from his bedstand, and I sipped slowly, feeling the first signs of life come back to me.

It took me a few additional moments before I could finally bring myself to ask, "You slept with someone?"

"Yes," he answered spitefully.

"Who?" I whispered, tears coming to my eyes, as if they were waiting for some fluids before they could gather.

"No one you know," he answered.

"Why?" I asked.

"I don't know … It just happened! I guess I was lonely."

I heard his words, but they angered me.

"Lonely?" I asked, not knowing how to take in his answer.

I felt the blood rush to my head and gathered the energy to get out of bed. The apartment felt small and claustrophobic.

I turned on automatic mode and put on the first thing I saw. Then I seized my cell phone from the kitchen counter, grabbed a bottle of water, slipped on my sneakers, and headed out toward the elevator, slamming the door shut behind me. My heart pounded, and adrenaline ran through my veins.

I suddenly realized it was the first time ever that I had walked out on Ben without saying a word. I comprehended there was no way back now and, for the first time ever, I felt lost in Japan.

My relationship with Ben had always seemed so solid to me. Even if we had a fight, I had always felt there was something to say, some way to get back to normal, even if it meant to contain his silent treatment or temporary rage on his end. With all our ups and downs, I had never thought infidelity would be an issue. I felt as if a part of my own body had betrayed me, as if I had suddenly become deformed without warning.

Why would Ben do that to me? I found myself standing in front of our building, saying these words in my mind again and again, not knowing where to go.

I took a few deep breaths and started walking. I didn't even know where to. I walked for hours without rest, waves of sorrow nearly drowning me from the inside. Tears of grief slid uncontrollably down my cheeks, leaving my lips salty. I avoided looking at the people passing by so as not to cause them any discomfort. I just kept on walking and walking aimlessly through a city of endless people with no one to ask where I should go or what I should do.

Whenever I looked up from the ground, I saw people moving with purpose. On the subway, in the underground tunnels, in restaurants, lavish department stores, and the little mom and pop shops, they all seemed to have found their answers. Under and over ground, in the endless floors of concrete corporate monstrosities, everything seemed to be pumping with life and meaning.

I was not only lost, I was empty and blank. I visited every shrine and temple I passed, clapping my hands dozens of times and calling out to any god or spirit willing to listen and provide me with direction. No one answered.

As evening fell, with its deep reds filling the autumn sky, I could no longer stand on my feet. I dragged myself home, battling internally with my deeper desire to simply disappear.

I walked in to find Ben sitting at our kitchen bar, a frail look on his face. He turned toward me, his eyes panicky like a mouse trapped in a maze.

Chapter 14: Redefining My Anchors

Getting back home that night, I felt sick to my stomach, but I knew I had to face him. I told him that he should stay until I figured things out. He didn't protest. I threw his pillow, a blanket, and some linen out beyond our bedroom door and into the living room and shut the door of our bedroom behind me. An atmosphere of mourning took over our home.

As autumn reached its peak and the bare, gray trees froze in place defenselessly, everywhere I looked, my vulnerabilities were being reflected back to me. I experienced great loneliness, especially in Ben's presence, and yet I was not ready to make any drastic decisions as to our future as a couple.

I was broken. I prayed that maybe one day I would find the strength to become whole again, to possibly forgive him. Until his betrayal, living far from the U.S. and from my parents, I had been comforted by clinging to the familiar, even if it was far from ideal … even if the price was high. With Ben, it certainly was. Now my familiar became an enigma; perhaps one I was afraid to confront. Keeping Ben there, even as hostage, prone to my inner battle, was the only thing I could manage.

The hardest part was to let go of; the most disturbing aspect of Ben's betrayal—my shattered trust. It had been the two of us against the world, or so I had wanted to believe. Ben had been my shelter when things got difficult, even if the shelter required heavy lifting. Moreover, Ben had been the last person on earth I could ever imagine cheating on me. It was simply too hard to accept the fact that it actually had happened. I knew that there were problems in our relationship, but it had simply never crossed my mind that trust was one of them. I knew there was an imbalance between us in terms of purpose, career, or occupation—whatever you chose to call it—but I had trusted that was his choice and that our relationship could contain it. The loneliness and confusion caused by Ben's unfaithfulness forced me to redefine new anchors, since Ben was no longer one of them.

There was no one I could come up with to replace the confidence I'd had in Ben. My parents were too far and too preoccupied with their own lives and, to be honest, I hadn't made any real friends in Japan.

It took me a few months until I finally understood that a clear routine at home would eventually allow me to become stronger. I thought that, only as an autonomous individual, independent from him, I could gather the strength to forgive him. I tried a variety of steps until I finally concluded what these anchors should be, and then I wrote them on a small piece of paper, which I slipped into my wallet and peeked at whenever I felt lost.

<u>Anchor list:</u>

1) Keep a clear routine at home.

2) Divide household tasks.
3) Avoid confrontations with Ben.
4) Avoid Ben altogether.
5) Strengthen work relationships.

Ben, for the most part, kept his head down. He was cooperative and patient, performing his share of household tasks according to my list of expectations promptly. He slept on the couch without objecting and stayed out of my way as much as possible. I assumed what kept him hopeful was the fact that we had dealt with pain together from the very start and had overcome some very dark days together. I assumed Ben took this into account and felt there could be an upside in the long-term, even if that meant investing in daily chores and in the short-term.

Soon after Ben and I had met for the first time at Taipei Airport, he had called to invite me for what he had phrased as, "A weekend down south, which you will never forget!" His voice had been very reassuring.

Six years had passed since that weekend down south, and I still remembered that weekend as if it were yesterday.

"A weekend down south?" I asked, quickly adding in a bit of a teasing tone. "But I still don't really know you!"

"No strings attached," Ben answered. "I just want you to see where I grew up. I want you to join me for a weekend at my grandparents' farm in Texas." It was undoubtedly one of the more original opening lines I had heard.

Spending a weekend with the grandparents had not sounded much of a romantic proposal, but that was what actually made it feel oddly right. There was something real and authentic about it.

Ben had picked me up from the local airport in his grandfather's light blue truck and, from the moment he had started driving, he had not stopped talking until we had reached the farm. I wasn't sure if he had just been nervous about having me there or whether he had been enthusiastically preparing the ground for our stay. Judging from his tone, it had been clear that his grandparents were a true source of pride for him. He had wanted me to know that they were both Holocaust survivors, atheists who were nonetheless thrilled about him bringing a Jewish girl over for the weekend. He had prepared me for his grandmother's tendency to break into song, mainly in Polish, at any given moment, as well as his grandfather's habit of introducing all twenty-two chickens on his farm by name.

Without a doubt, he had prepared me well, and I had felt at home from the moment we'd arrived. I had found the two of them both entertaining and inspiring, just as Ben had portrayed them.

Ben's grandfather had been dressed in a simple white T-shirt and a pair of old khaki pants, and as soon as we had arrived, he had put on Yiddish music, playing it loudly as if it were heavy metal and as if it would impress his young lady guest. Raising his hands in the air and moving to the traditional music, he had called his wife to join him. I could see the power of life in his eyes, and Ben and I could not detach our eyes from them. We had watched them, amused. Then had come the royal tour of the farm and, just as Ben had predicted, his grandfather had shared with me the names of all his chickens from largest to smallest.

As daylight had faded over the farm, Ben's grandfather's

energy had slowly ebbed, and he had transformed into a storyteller, heavily rooted in his large, red armchair. He had told us about how he had fled Poland when he had only been sixteen, and how he had gone underground, arranging fake passports for Jewish refugees from all across Europe. He had gone into details of his capture and jailing in Egypt on his way to the Holy land, how he had eventually migrated to the U.S., and how he had searched years for his siblings and parents, who he had never seen again.

Ben's grandmother, on the other hand, with her soft, blue eyes, had appeared happy to be an observer of stories that she had no doubt heard endless times. Yet, knowing they were being revealed to us seemed to have caused her pleasure. All in all, she had seemed excited that two young people had chosen to spend a weekend with them at their notable age, as if she had been witnessing a visit from a distinguished diplomatic mission. She had complimented me nonstop as to confirm her approval to Ben, which was no trivial matter, as she herself had seemed to have a secret infatuation with her grandson. Every time Ben had passed by in his shorts, she would lean over in my direction and whisper, "Have you ever seen such beautiful legs?"

On the second day of my visit, we had woken to the sound of Ben's grandmother charmingly singing. As soon as I had shown up in the dining room, Ben's grandfather had grabbed my hand with a strong affirmative grip and pulled me toward the kitchen counter. He had then spent half the morning showing me how the toaster worked, putting slices of bread in and popping the toast out, amused each time it had, one piece after the other.

"Perfect, aren't they? What our technology can do today!" he said enthusiastically as he took each slice out, examining it from all angles before carefully spreading it with butter.

Sharing his enthusiasm for the wonders of a twenty-first century toaster had seemed like the right thing to do. I'd assumed landing on the moon would have been on the top of his list, but I might have been a bit naïve. All in all, that had been one of the most magical, most meaningful weekends I had had, and Ben had most definitely given me a unique and significant peek into his soul and roots.

A few months later, in June, Tropical Storm Allison had hit. Without warning, as tropical storms went, it had destroyed Ben's grandparents' farm. Watching the news, I had felt devastated for them. However, what had actually upset them the most was the idea that a natural disaster had erased any trace of the self-sustaining environment they'd succeeded in building for themselves after surviving the horrors of the Holocaust. This feeling that they hadn't been spared of evidently losing their home and dignity shattered their spirits, as if the Nazis had finally caught up with them.

Ben's grandfather's heart had soon failed while watching the movie *Schindler's List* on Ben's parents' DVD player for the sixteenth time in three weeks. Ben's grandmother, the devoted farmer's wife, had gone to sleep heartbroken on the last night of her husband's *shiva* and had never woken up.

With the death of Ben's grandfather, Ben had seemed lost in a great cloud of darkness, and although we had kept a long-distance relationship until then, hearing his voice over the phone, I had understood that I needed to fly in to be beside him for the full week of his grandfather's *shiva*. I then, of course, had found myself staying an additional week for the *shiva* of his grandmother. *Talk about intense*!

Having known Ben's grandparents, albeit for only one weekend, had made me feel, for the first time in my life, that being Jewish wasn't just about conforming to the basic traditions but rather a heritage I shouldn't deny but embrace, if not for my own sake than for the sake of those who had lost their lives for simply being born Jewish. I had felt that, were I ever to marry Ben, the fact that he was the grandson of Holocaust survivors would make it all the more meaningful. That thought had met me numerous times during our years together, and even now, with all my pain.

I also understood their fervent wish for him to marry a Jewish woman, and not from religious motives, as the encounter with them had strengthened something much more subtle in my connection with my Jewish identity. In fact, if you had ever mentioned God to Ben's grandfather, he would have probably smiled and gently explained, as if talking to a child, that the Holocaust was proof that there was no God.

Just a few months after we had finished mourning those two significant individuals, tragedy had struck again. This time, it had come from my end.

Naomi, the firefighter and my best friend from childhood, had been on her way to meet Michelle, her girlfriend who was some sort of financial wiz working at the New York Stock Exchange. Having not seen Michelle all weekend due to Naomi's grueling shifts at the station, Naomi had decided to surprise Michelle at her office in Lower Manhattan. Naomi had rarely fallen for anyone. She had been, after all, a redheaded free spirit.

"Michelle is different!" she told me over the phone the last time we had spoken, and I had felt that perhaps she had found love for the first time.

On her way to Michelle's office, Naomi had stopped at a deli to grab bagels and coffee, and then, turning the corner, she had witnessed the first plane hit the Twin Towers.

Eyewitnesses said they had seen Naomi run straight into the cloud of ash, relentlessly passing through the confused crowd while directing people away from the danger. Although off firefighting duty that day, Naomi had last been seen running deeper into what had already been hit by an additional plane and would later become known as Ground Zero.

The news of her loss had been overwhelming; perhaps the most overwhelming experience I had ever felt. I had felt the shock, the denial, that panic, anger, frustration, and finally a sadness I had never known could exist within me. Add to that the shock from the whole morbid attack on U.S. soil, it had made Ben and I feel as if nowhere was safe and nothing would ever be certain again. It was as if we were filling a puzzle containing pieces of our lives yet had no board to work on, and so some pieces just broke off into the emptiness, leaving the image of our own reality full of unknown and unrecoverable blanks.

The fact that I had lost Naomi, and he had lost his grandparents in such a short time period, truly challenged my belief in good over evil, as well as my faith in humanity, in justice, and in God. We had experienced so much loss, yet life just went on, despite the fact that it made no sense. We had been filled with pain and darkness. The thought of moving on had seemed so unbearable. Having Ben's arms around me as my head sunk into his chest had been the closest thing I had to feeling sheltered and protected.

Though relatively new to each other, this intense period under such unexpected and extreme circumstances, with two proceeding shivas, followed by the loss of my best friend, initiated a bond that had tied us together in a transcending union of continuous grief.

If I had to map out the path from the day that Ben and I had met to before I knew of his betrayal, I would emphasize trust as our bedrock, or the main asset that we marched on from the very start. Our first few months together had been characterized by despair and tragedy, exposing our true weaknesses, our undisguised selves, and strengthening our mutual dependency. A bond built on a longing for solid ground in an unpredictable world, we had transplanted our roots into one another and had protected each other as if we were one and the same.

I assumed that this bond had kept me fighting my way through Ben's endless episodes and mood shifts. I had felt it was my mission to stay strong, as if he had nothing in the world to depend on other than my tolerance and embrace at any cost.

Within the first six months of our acquaintance, Ben and I had dealt with so much pain that we had keenly believed things could only get better. We had an enhanced sense of security that, if we made it together through these dark days and nights, we could survive any challenge that life threw at us, as long as we were together. This sense of security had soon been complemented by strong feelings of loyalty, which in turn became what I had considered love.

Chapter 15: Playing Barbie

The icicles in my blood had officially made it the coldest winter ever. Ben and I were managing to maintain a relationship composed of zero drama; his infidelity remaining unmentioned as it was still too painful for me to confront. Then, this evening, I was supposed to go out to dinner with a client, but due to a sudden crisis at one of his factories in the south, the meeting had been canceled. *I am so relieved.*

Dark and cold days were not my favorite for outing on the town. All I really wanted was to go home. The thought of crawling into bed with a cup of hot chocolate and a good romantic, Hollywood comedy dubbed in Japanese seemed like the perfect end to a cold, gloomy day. The truth was that these romantic comedies were considerably less romantic but undeniably funnier when dubbed in Japanese.

The subway home was packed, but luckily, a few stops along, I snatched a seat. I took off my coat and placed it on my knees since the gap in temperature was unreal between outside and within the subway.

I looked up to read the ads above the seats across from me when I saw Rachel Levin standing by the door, gazing out toward the tracks. I stared at her for a few seconds and felt my hands begin to sweat. Then, without any warning, it hit me.

It was Rachel! She's the one Ben slept with. It must be her! I had suspected something was off the previous times that I had seen her on our train. All that time, Ben had said he was interviewing her for his book … I should have figured it out. *It makes perfect sense. She is one of the very few people not on Ben's blacklist. She is sweet and petite, and Ben always laughs at her cutesy comments as if she is his little pet tamagochi.*

And her truly wanting Noah? For real? I could never understand how Ben finds her so funny. And she talks so much! Ben usually hates people who babble on and on …

How did I not see this before?

I pulled off my scarf as I felt the heat take over me. *I am going to suffocate.* I closed my eyes and tried to slow down my breathing, counting to four while inhaling and four while exhaling, trying to get a grip on the anxiety that was rapidly taking over me.

When we finally arrived at our station and the sliding doors opened, Rachel stepped out casually onto the platform. I pushed my way out of the subway, feeling I could not control the anger building up inside me.

As she headed toward the escalator, I headed farther down the platform, and then I ran up the steps with ice-cold wind blowing at me, both my coat and scarf still in my hands. By the time we both reached ground level, I was breathless, sweaty, and cold, yet Rachel seemed in no hurry at all. She stood at the top of the escalator, pulling her hair back and talking offhandedly on her cell phone.

I quickly hid behind the supervisor's booth and put on my coat and scarf, freezing at the tip of my nose.

As Rachel put her cell phone away, my body shifted into high alert. As soon as she started walking toward the exit gate, I tailed along behind her.

Although I would have placed a huge bet on her walking in the direction of our apartment building to meet with Ben, who was not yet aware of the fact that the dinner with my client had been canceled, she instead turned left, the opposite direction of our home.

Perhaps she had noticed me before I had noticed her, and perhaps she had been talking to Ben on the phone, and he had suggested they change the location of their meeting.

Just as I was about to leap out in her direction, a voice from within brought me back to my senses.

Stop! You are obviously paranoid! Ben deeply regrets what he did. Even if it was Rachel, there is no way they are still having an affair! You have to learn to trust Ben again ...

Regardless, before I could stop, I still found myself running after *her*.

I soon saw her silhouette before me, and I wanted to paint her crimson and slap a big "A" on her chest for adulterer. The farther Rachel got from the station, the faster her pace got. At a certain point, she turned the corner, and I sensed she had realized I was following her. But then, a few blocks later, she started slowing down. Finally, she stopped. She looked in both directions then swiftly entered the gate of a cemetery. *Of all places? A cemetery?*

Okay, I am not paranoid. What a great coverup! The ideal place to meet Ben! Brilliant!

I continued through the gate, following her closely like an old-time detective. Every few steps, I stopped and pretended to be texting, picking up a leaf, or kneeling by a grave. *If I am lucky enough, I will come across one of those tall family graves where I can hide and rest for a moment. It wouldn't hurt the Japanese to have some tall tombstones once in a while*, I told myself, dusting my knees for the umpteenth time.

Then Rachel came to an abrupt stop, and I froze in place, hoping she hadn't noticed me. There was total silence, and I waited tensely as Rachel slowly turned around and stood in front of a garden with little stone statues.

Where is Ben? I asked myself, assuming she was wondering the same …

A few moments passed, and then she knelt beside one of the tiny stone statues. I looked at her attentively. There was something unfamiliar in her posture, in the way she moved gently, pushing her hair back, looking thoughtfully at the stone statue. Then she suddenly reached out to her fancy Fendi handbag. I was mesmerized as she searched for something, probably her cell phone—perhaps Ben was keeping her waiting too long. Then she seemed to have found it in her bag and, in an instant, her body language changed, and she was back to being the same Rachel Levin I knew.

Just as I thought I could read her again—and assuming she was just about to pull out her cell phone and call Ben—without any warning whatsoever, she pulled out an unimaginably adorable, baby-sized sweater.

What the …?

I watched Rachel *dress* the statue.

This is too weird.

I leaned forward, trying to get a better view of what was going on in front of me, and I nearly tripped over. Creepy did not even begin to describe what I was witnessing. I stared, stunned.

A second glance, and it seemed it was not the first statue in the cemetery that had been "played Barbie" with … No.

I was speechless—well, just for a moment—then my mind went all over the place.

Our sweet, darling Rachel dressing up a stone statue in a graveyard—how dark and morbid! Maybe Noah and Ben should simply get a glance at this and, finally, they won't stare at her with those puppy eyes, almost begging her to pet them. Or maybe she has pet them—I mean, Ben. Who knows? Maybe she even slapped him and dressed him up as Ken? Ew.

I felt dizzy and leaned back, closing my eyes and trying to stop the noise in my head.

Finally, I pulled myself together. I was starting to feel a bit weird about this whole Sherlock Holmes situation. I assumed, by now, that Ben was not coming and felt a bit guilty about the fact that I now knew her secret—or her madness. Maybe one of the two, or even both. I couldn't figure out yet which one it was … but it was dark.

And it was freezing. I tightened my scarf and quietly headed out of the cemetery to go home.

Ben was there when I arrived, staring quietly at me when I walked in, as he did every evening, as if waiting for me to declare peace. I could hardly look at him from shame, and I dared not mention a thing to him about following Rachel to the cemetery, determined to blow his cover, convinced that they had or still were having an affair.

Over the next few days, the image of Rachel dressing the miniature statue at the cemetery was the first thing that went through my mind when I woke up and the last thing I thought of before I fell asleep.

Chapter 16: Anchor #5

As the world turned around me, and though I had managed to find relative stability at home with our detached routine, I realized I still needed, now even more than ever, someone I could talk with. Finally, I decided it was Yuki, my fifth anchor, a colleague I could talk with.

"Oh no! I left my employee badge on my desk …" I called out to Yuki on our way down for curry with the boys, hoping he would tell them to go ahead and offer to wait for me. He did. *First step concluded.*

I headed back to our cubicle. At my desk, I shifted some piles of paper around, trying to give the impression that I was looking for something. At a certain point, Rie, the third member of our cubicle, stared at me with a big question mark on her face. I shot a look back at her and smiled.

I don't think I have ever heard Rie open her mouth. The thought crossed my mind. *I wonder whether there is any chance that, if I continue with the paper shifting and make even louder and more annoying noises, she will eventually snap, and I will finally hear her voice ...* I entertained myself for a moment with that thought then remembered Yuki was waiting for me near the elevator.

I snatched the employee badge then headed back to him, my heart racing with the thought of finally sharing part of my burden with someone.

The doors of the elevator shut on the two of us and, without warning, it all simply spilled out. I told Yuki *everything*, from Ben's confession to Rachel's freak show at the cemetery. Miraculously, it all took me less than seven minutes, which was the exact time it took to get from our office elevators to the curry joint.

As we reached the joint, I concluded my rapid review, pushed my shades up, turned to Yuki with a curious and helpless smile, and asked, "So, what do you think?"

Yuki lifted his shades, as well, and released a sympathetic smile back at me. Unlike most other Japanese I knew, Yuki was relatively direct and allowed himself to skip the conversational foreplay in some situations. Still, like most Japanese, he was typically wary of making judgments.

I watched him carefully weigh his words before he finally began.

"About you following Rachel, I would have done exactly the same thing," he said.

Wow, what a relief! My shoulders released some of their tension, and the creases on my forehead began to unfold. *Yuki is definitely my fifth anchor!* I told myself, inhaling deeply and exhaling into a wide, panoramic smile.

But just as I started to unwind, Yuki placed one hand behind his neck.

Oh no! I must have crossed the line! This usually signals a warning of too much personal information for a Japanese to digest without an alcoholic drink or two!

The alarms started squealing in my head. It was actually Yuki who had taught me the meaning of the hand-behind-the-neck gesture.

It turned out that, for my first couple of months in the division, I had asked Mr. Kobayashi some inappropriate questions, always assuming from his lack of response that he just hadn't heard me or had simply chosen to avoid my questions. One day, Yuki had taken me aside, as he could no longer watch this cross-cultural barrier between Mr. Kobayashi and me repeat itself. He had explained to me that, as soon as a Japanese individual put his hand behind his neck, in the midst of a dialogue, the agreed upon code of conduct was to simply drop the subject. In other words, it meant *please back off*.

The alarms in my head got stronger. *I can't lose Yuki as my anchor!* In a culture where conflict tended to be avoided, you needed to know how to read the signs.

Just as I was starting to regret sharing my telenovela, Yuki finally continued, "Your friend isn't crazy; don't worry. These tiny statues are for children who died or were made to die before they were born. She was probably hoping that the spirit of the unborn baby will forgive her. That's why she visits it, dresses it, and shares her love toward it."

I stared at Yuki incredulously. *Are you for real?* were the first words that crossed my mind. Then again, it wasn't the first time I had been left speechless after learning something new about the Japanese. I could understand why he had taken so long and how the topic had made him uncomfortable. And as to what he had just told me, I didn't know what seemed odder—the notion that Japanese people dressed up stone statues at cemeteries or the thought that Rachel had had an abortion. I knew that she and Noah were thinking of starting a family. They were waiting until his relocation next year to a closer office instead of him taking two-hour commutes in each direction with a baby at home. *But there's no way she would have an abortion if she got pregnant before.*

I thanked Yuki for his candid answer and apologized for any discomfort I might have caused him. He smiled back sympathetically.

"I'm not actually that hungry anymore," I told him, pushing my sunglasses back over my eyes, trying to keep it together and not cause him any discomfort by sharing my confusion.

He walked in to join the boys, and I returned to the office. A part of me felt relieved that there was finally someone out there who knew what I was going through. Another part of me was still slightly ashamed to have put a Japanese through a *hand behind the neck* situation.

As I returned to the office, my feet got heavier. Nothing made sense anymore. I reached my cubicle, put the papers back where they should have been, and laid my cell phone and employee badge on top of them. I sat down, elbows on the desk, head in hands. I had no idea what to think any longer.

Then I was struck by a disturbing notion that seemed to have popped up for a second when Yuki had spoken but was then pushed aside. *Maybe the baby wasn't Noah's! Maybe Rachel had an affair and got pregnant, and then had an abortion ... Maybe it was Ben's?*

I felt as if someone had pushed a knife through my chest.

I didn't dare share this last bit with Yuki, realizing that my anchor might need a rest from all the drama.

I smiled at him when he returned from lunch, and his eyes reassured me that my secrets were safe with him. Then I somehow survived the day at the office, although I could feel Rie's eyes on me at all times as I fidgeted under my desk.

On my way home from the station, I felt empty, stupid, angry, numb. At the entrance to our building, I forced myself to walk in, reluctantly stepping into the elevator. As the doors shut, I took a deep breath, closed my eyes, and prayed for the unlikely possibility that Ben wasn't home. My prayer was heard. I was spared. For now.

Chapter 17: Regrets

Three days later, I found myself storming into the living room, unable to control myself any longer.

"Was it Rachel?" I asked, getting right to the point.

"Was what Rachel?" he answered, not having expected me to even speak to him.

"Were you sleeping with Rachel?" I elaborated unwillingly.

"Are you insane?"

"I know she had an abortion. Was the baby yours?" I simply spilled it all out.

There was silence, and I could see that Ben was struggling to keep something from me.

"So it *is* true!" I finally yelled at him, breaking the silence.

"It's not what you think," he answered, but his choice of a textbook answer just pushed me over the edge.

"What the hell, Ben? Rachel? Really?" I shouted louder.

"Sarah, relax. I'm telling you the truth; it's not what you think," he repeated in an even more controlled voice, which I found both patronizing and insulting.

I grabbed my bag and coat then headed for the front door.

Just as I was about to open it, Ben called out, "Sarah, stop!" and shoved his yellow novel notes between the door and my face. "Read this page."

The fact that Ben was proffering his yellow notes was no minor event; they had always been for his eyes only.

I stepped back slowly and turned to examine his eyes. He stared straight back at me. Then I snatched the yellow notepad out of his hands and marched into the bedroom, shutting the door behind me.

> *Summary of R's life story (highly confidential!)*
>
> *R was raised in Kyoto and graduated from Kyoto University, where she met her first serious boyfriend, Toru. She's the only child of a well-respected mayor from the Kansai area.*
>
> *When R started seeing Toru, her father, concerned for his own political image, ran a background check on him, revealing that Toru was descended from an outcast community called the Burakumin. Though many Japanese would deny it, there is still quite a bit of prejudice against them.*
>
> *R's father demanded that she stop seeing Toru, but she secretly continued her relationship with him for three more years, until the day she realized she was pregnant. Knowing her father would never forgive her,*

she decided to tell her mother, who she knew would do everything to protect her, both from her father and from public shame.

R's mother sent her to Tokyo for an abortion and set her up with a Buddhist priest who offered her a stone statue to appease the soul of her unborn baby.

A year after moving to Tokyo, R married another man, hoping for a fresh start. Her biggest fear is that the soul of her aborted child will punish her, and that she may never get pregnant again ...

I couldn't breathe. I put the notes down on the bed. It was a lot to take in—everything I had built up in my head had simply been a misunderstanding, and I realized I'd put Ben in an incredibly difficult position.

I was quite certain that Ben was one of the few people who knew Rachel's story. He had that gift of getting people to tell him their utmost secrets in confidence, and now I had forced him to betray her trust.

I took another deep breath then went out into the living room. Ben was perched on the sofa, waiting for my response. I came closer to him, and he straightened, his eyes examining mine. I slowly lifted my arms and hugged him.

"I'm sorry," I whispered to him.

"I'm sorry," he answered. "This was not mine to share. I kept the notes simply for inspiration. I understand that you still can't trust me, so I can't blame you for suspecting me. And I don't even understand how you made this connection,"

Ben added quietly. I could feel his shoulders loosen with relief as he hugged me back. "I can't stand the thought of losing you." He hugged me tighter.

I stepped back. I might have led him to believe things had now changed between us, but the truth was I was not quite ready yet to get into the issues concerning our relationship and to consider forgiving him.

Ben examined me carefully then he let his head fall silently, disappointed that we hadn't made the progress he had been hoping for.

I put the notes down on the sofa and went back to the bedroom, closing the door behind me.

Chapter 18: Rock Star

While I was at last convinced that Ben was truly sorry, I was still far from letting go of my anger. Having read his notes and learning Rachel's sad story, I actually began to enjoy Noah and Rachel's company more than before. Yes, we reinitiated our rare social engagements, not to isolate ourselves completely, and were able to put a sufficient act on—or so I believed.

The fact that Rachel had more substance than what met the eye made me more sympathetic and tolerant toward her giggly behavior. I also felt a special bond with her as we were both embracing unspoken betrayals—her of her father's trust and of Toru's love—and have redefined our anchors in order to move on.

The hug that evening was the last physical contact Ben and I had for the next few months. It was actually the only physical contact we had had since his confession. He woke up every morning, looking at me with cautious optimism that perhaps the time had come and I had found a way to forgive him. But I still wanted very little contact with him. It wasn't a conscious decision; it was something deeper, more primitive than that, perhaps some sort of protective mechanism. On the one hand, I felt he had become a total stranger living with me in my home, yet I didn't feel that I was ready to let him go. So, I worked and worked and worked, never looking at my watch and never leaving the office early. I understood that, no matter who Ben had slept with, I still needed time to figure things out.

During the coldest winter nights, one dream kept recurring, waking me up with a face bathed in sweat and a heart beating with anxiety. In the dream, it was mid-summer. The sun was just setting, and the sky was ablaze with heartwarming shades of red. I was on my way home from work and passed the 7-Eleven and the pharmacy, just like any other day. Wherever I looked, people seemed cheerful and friendly. Then I passed Mrs. Toda's temple, and I heard a commotion coming from within her gate. It was much louder than that time when Dharma had gone missing.

As I carefully pushed the gate open, the noise stopped abruptly. And instead of Mrs. Toda's temple, I found an open field, with rows and rows of sunflowers. The sunflowers were exceptionally tall, almost my height.

I entered the field, drawn in by a warm, comforting sensation, and just as I was about to succumb to its magical calling, the commotion started up again. I looked around me, but all I saw were the tall, proud, silent yellow flowers. I suddenly realized that the noise was coming from beneath the flowers.

I knelt down and discovered that I was surrounded by hundreds of miniature stone statues, similar to the one I had seen Rachel dress at the cemetery. Torn between the desire to run and the need to understand the source of the turmoil, I froze. Chills crept up my spine as I realize that the statues were generating the sounds of crying newborns. One statue in particular caught my attention. As I looked closer, I noticed that the tiny stone figure had Ben's face on it! I looked around, suddenly aware that they all carried Ben's face.

I pulled a pacifier out of my pocket and turned back to the first statue that had caught my attention. But just as I was about to put the pacifier in its mouth, the statue's face transformed into the face of the "Sweaty Swine" from the Japanese automotive company. I pulled back and tried to get away, but he snatched the pacifier out of my hand and shoved it into my mouth.

I was fixed to the spot while he yelled at me, "And you think you understand the Japanese spirit?"

The dream was so surreal and so detailed that, every time I dreamt it, I was astonished anew by the chain of events. Its themes, however, were no great surprise. Just as my personal life came crashing down, the transaction between the Japanese and Europeans started going downhill, as well.

It turned out that when the Silky-Haired Tap Dancer in Disguise had claimed a personal emergency during my last trip to Europe, it had been no false alarm or lame excuse to postpone negotiations. He had actually had an urgent personal matter. His wife—yes, he had a wife, which I still found hard to picture—had gone into premature labor, on the subway of all places! She had been taken to the nearest hospital and evidently had lost a lot of blood. Once stabilized, she'd had a caesarean section, leaving her an additional two months in the hospital together with their twin preemies. The Europeans, not wanting to be too insensitive by replacing him too soon, had simply put things on hold.

Finally, a week ago, we had been notified that the position of Head of Negotiations for the European team had been transferred to someone new named Tom Weber.

Mr. Kobayashi, the typical risk averse Japanese, was stressed by the transition, realizing he had to invest in a new relationship. The Japanese automotive team, on the other hand, did not appear to mind the delay, and Mr. Inui even seemed quite pleased by the thought of a replacement of his European silky-haired counterpart.

My day did not start out that great. First, I woke up at 3:30 a.m. in a panic from my recurring dream. After drying the cold sweat from my forehead, I looked out at Tokyo Tower, eager to see a hint of daylight. It was still pitch dark.

A few failed attempts to get back to sleep, and I finally heaved myself out into the kitchen. As I passed the sofa, I caught a glimpse of Ben sleeping. I was envious of his ability to sleep so peacefully, while I was haunted by grotesque images of his face on screaming statues night after night. Watching him made me feel all the more depressed.

I moved to the kitchen and pulled a glass out of the cupboard. I made no special efforts to keep quiet, my envy transforming into anger. I filled the glass with water and, as I took my first sip, I was suddenly flooded with emotion. With my second sip, I was on the kitchen floor, sobbing big, wet tears. It was the first time I had really cried out loud since Ben's confession. The more I cried, the louder I got, mainly because I was so upset that Ben, just a few feet away, kept on sleeping like a baby.

It was about 5:00 a.m. when I finally pulled myself together and dragged myself to the bathroom where I filled up our deep, square-shaped bath. *Yes, square-shaped! What were they thinking? The whole idea of a bath is to spread yourself out, feet up, head back ... But no, the Japanese had to make it square!*

I stepped into the square bath, grabbing the notes I had prepared for the meeting with Mr. Weber. I looked at them and realized I was lacking the energy to read even a single word.

At 7:15, I left for work, and Ben was still peacefully asleep.

On the ground floor of our office building, from my bag, I pulled out one of my favorite Japanese inventions—mint-flavored eye drops that took the red out of your eyes while generating a mint-rush to the head, similar to a wasabi-rush. Brilliant. In my opinion, they were a must-have for any business professional lacking sleep or attending a meeting after an emotional breakdown.

I stared into the gold mirrored wall separating the two lobby elevators, and just as I tipped my head back to soak in the first drop of my magical remedy, a Gucci-type Ms. Perfect stormed out of one of the elevators. She was stunning, but more than that, she looked really familiar. It should be stressed that, in Japan, women do not usually storm out of anywhere. Japanese women either strolled out in a cute, girlish fashion, exited quietly with elegance, or retreated gracefully with tiny, mincing steps like well-trained geishas. Storming out and, thereby, attracting the attention of hungover, 9:00 a.m. Japanese businessmen was uncommon, to say the least. Even

I found myself bewildered by Ms. Perfect's striking debut.

As soon as I walked through the glass doors into our division, Yuki filled me in on the gossip. Turned out that I recognized Ms. Perfect from one of the popular Japanese TV dramas. She had been visiting none other than our office before storming out of the elevator in the lobby. Apparently, she'd had some sort of drama with Mr. Kobayashi in our meeting room. *Yes, Mr. Kobayashi, my boss—the humdrum, corporate, grey-suited, boring, predictable, please-all, conservative Japanese boss.* She was allegedly the more verbal; that at least suited the profile. I would never have thought tight-assed Mr. Kobayashi capable of surviving an argument, but I guessed you had to hand it to her—after all, she was a TV drama star.

Anyhow, no one really knew what had gone on in the meeting room or the nature of the relationship between the two. *She must be at least twenty years younger than him.* We had met his wife and son last spring at our corporate cherry blossom party, and they had looked like quite a happy, normal family. But I was probably being naïve, as usual. *If Ben can be unfaithful to me, why couldn't Mr. Kobayashi be having an affair with a drama queen half his age? Maybe she is just what he needs to blow off some steam ...*

Oh my God, I cannot believe I'm actually starting to think like a man ...

Mr. Inui and his automotive team arrived ten minutes early and waited patiently in the meeting room. Mr. Kobayashi was simply not himself. Whatever had happened with Ms. Perfect must have really upset him.

Mr. Weber and his team showed up right on time.

Astonishingly, Mr. Weber was wearing neither a jacket nor a tie. He entered the room, introduced himself as Tom, and then collected everyone's business cards, shoving them into the pockets of his khaki cargo pants. Before anyone could respond, Tom then sat down, crossed his legs, knocked off his slippers, and declared, "We need to figure out if this whole merger thing is just a waste of our time."

Wowza! Not one of these! I could feel myself panicking slightly, mainly that Mr. Kobayashi lived through the day.

The room went silent. Everyone froze, staring at Tom, as if perhaps they had misunderstood his English.

As if that was not enough, he then continued with, "So, are we in or are we out?"

He is *one of those*, I confirmed to myself, unable to take my eyes off him.

No one moved an inch.

Mr. Inui, across the table from Tom, carefully observed the young man who dared to show up and dismiss three years of his meticulous hard work. Mr. Kobayashi, sitting between Mr. Inui and me, remained perfectly still. I could feel Mr. Kobayashi's body temperature rise, and I could picture how both sides of his forehead were starting to show those long, symmetrical signs of sweat, as often happened when he got worked up. All the others just sat in silence, as if awaiting a fatal duel in an old-time western.

"Oh, those Europeans and their sense of humor!" I finally said as convincingly as I could, forcing a tiny laugh.

All eyes shifted in my direction and heads turned diagonally. A few seconds later, the tension lifted, and the Japanese team burst out in a polite, unified wave of laughter.

Now Tom seemed slightly confused.

"So, Tom," I took the lead, covering up for Mr. Kobayashi's lack of response, "we will be delighted to fill you in on all the details, but first off, we would like to invite you and your team for dinner and some Japanese-style entertainment this evening."

The room remained mute. Even Tom got the feeling that a silent coup might be taking place.

"How about we enjoy some Japanese food and rock music?" I finally suggested, hoping that rock music would perhaps limit the need for discussion should the Japanese remain nonverbal throughout the evening.

Amused by my own improvisation techniques, I topped it off with my final knockout. "Tom, you seem like a guy who would appreciate rock music. Any chance you were in a band when you were young?"

Tom looked at me, rather baffled and a bit annoyed by my odd remark. He also seemed somewhat taken aback by the fact that I had taken over the conversation, helping avoid the matters that he had opened the meeting with. His slow reaction, however, did not do him justice because, before he could deny it, the Japanese let out a unanimous, "Aaah!" The basic sound they generated when they were profoundly impressed.

Tom looked around, trying to work out where this was heading, but before he could refute my wild claim that he himself might have been a rocker, Mr. Kobayashi, at long last, joined the discussion and asked in a courteous yet curious tone, "Tom-san, what instrument did you play in your rock band?"

In utter disbelief, though shaking his head, Tom finally answered, "Guitar." He was probably hoping that, with this, he would put an end to the ridiculous, fictitious plot that he was being forced to go along with.

"Aaah!" the Japanese responded unanimously.

At this point, it seemed Tom might have had enough. He stiffened and laid his elbows down on the table, ready for a fight, but just as he opened his mouth, the room began to shake or, in simple English, an earthquake took place. The timing could not have been more perfect. It was as if the divine spirits were enjoying Tom and my little game and didn't want Tom to ruin it for everyone else.

Legend had it that the Mongols had been drowned on the shores of Japan in a typhoon on their way to conquer Japan, courtesy of the divine spirits. *So, what's a little earthquake to save our merger?*

Once the room stopped shaking, Mr. Kobayashi, with his quick martial art instincts, flipped across the table and moved Tom's elbow to save him from staining his sleeve on some spilled tea.

Tom sat back, his eyes scanning the room, then fixed his gaze on Mr. Kobayashi. Despite the fact that his mouth was half-open, he seemed speechless.

Mr. Kobayashi finally took charge and declared, "Tom-san, we apologize for the earthquake. Why don't you and your team return to your hotel and get some rest and relax? We will all meet in the evening for your welcome dinner. And tomorrow, we can start talking about business."

Tom stood from his seat, seeming a bit in shock and still speechless. Earthquakes could have that effect.

He and his team left the room in silence, accompanied by Mr. Kobayashi, and bowed-off by myself and the Japanese team. I closed my notebook in relief and turned toward Mr. Inui with a cautious smile.

"In Japan, even rock stars show respect," said Mr. Inui, getting up and straightening the lapels of his suit.

"I know. I am sorry," I replied, as if I had the authority to apologize on behalf of all non-Japanese.

"You and Mr. Kobayashi have one week to try to fix things. If not, as your European friend put it, 'we will be out!' " He stormed out of the room, his team bowing apologetically to Mr. Kobayashi and me, and then they, too, left quickly to catch up with him.

After everyone was gone, I gathered my things then looked for Mr. Kobayashi. I found him standing behind his desk, gazing out the window. I could see by his posture that something haunted him, and it was greater than what had happened in the meeting just now. For the first time, there was something vulnerable about him that I did not recognize.

It wasn't that anxiety that took over him when business went south—that I'd learned to recognize and contain. It seemed that something more personal had hit him. I couldn't help but ask myself if it had anything to do with his meeting with Ms. Perfect, as if she had taken him emotionally to a faraway place, and she couldn't have chosen a worse day to do so. Yet, I could not imagine what they could have in common, nor what anyone could be so angry with Mr. Kobayashi about. *Perhaps she has decided to blackmail Mr. Kobayashi, following a failing affair? Or maybe she doesn't need him any longer, and he is heartbroken? Hmm ... that could take some time to get over.*

I tried to figure out how I was going to deal with Tom while trying to soothe Mr. Inui's distress. For the first time since joining the division, I felt that Mr. Kobayashi truly needed me to be there for him and to do what I needed to do. The only thing that was crystal clear to me was that we had one week to make things right or the Japanese would opt out.

Chapter 19: Dangerous Woman

Early in the evening, I picked the European team up from their hotel and noticed Tom making an effort to be friendlier. I assumed, amused from the image in my mind, that the box of expensive chocolates I had sent to his room had something to do with it. Or perhaps it was the note:

> *Dear Mr. Weber,*
> *I hope you recovered from the earthquake earlier today. The Japanese spirits have spoken. It seems your approach to your Japanese counterparts upset them. A small piece of advice: do not underestimate your Japanese partners nor the Japanese spirits. I will pick you up at six p.m. Don't be late.*
>
> *Enjoy your chocolates,*
> *Sarah*
>
> *P.S. I also played the guitar before I got in trouble with the Yakuza and ended up*

> *having to get a fake thumb. Beware—you've been warned!*

In the meantime, Mr. Kobayashi had volunteered Yuki and some other young bloods from our division to join our small dinner party.

We all met up, together with Mr. Inui and his team, at the entrance of a fancy dinner club. And, as soon as we entered, Mr. Kobayashi asked Tom to take a seat beside him, introducing him to the waitress as "a European rock star."

The waitress, in turn, responded with an inevitable, "Aaah!" and everyone laughed, even Tom.

Mr. Inui beckoned me to the seat next to him, and the truth was that I was relieved by his change of heart. I took a quick look in Mr. Kobayashi's direction, and he seemed pleased, as well.

We were served endless quantities of superb Japanese dishes and listened to loud Japanese rock music. The atmosphere was relaxed, and we simply enjoyed not talking business and, more so, not talking at all.

When the time came to move from beer to *saké*, Mr. Kobayashi took charge of the pouring. Once everyone else had been served, I held out my small ceramic cup with two hands and allowed Mr. Kobayashi to fill it up. *I love warm saké*, I thought, as the unique sensation passed my lips, filled my mouth, and coated my throat with warmness.

But, just as I started to unwind, a large, sweaty hand made its way up my thigh.

I cried out in my head, and the previously comforting sensation of *saké* transformed into a sharp sting in my throat.

I quickly collected myself and decided on: *Survival Scenario #1*. Previous encounters had taught me to always have escape strategies lined up just in case.

I reached out to the *saké* bottle and suggested filling up Mr. Inui's cup. As custom required, he reached over to his *saké* cup, releasing my thigh. Then I quietly leaned over toward him and whispered in a friendly voice, "We are going to play a little game."

Japanese adults actually do play games at social events. I know it's weird, but so is sweet red bean pudding for dessert, and they love that, too. Now we would see where Jewish Sunday school started paying off.

"Okay, the game goes like this," I start, eager to waste no time. "You know I am Jewish and that some Jews can even speak Hebrew. I will teach you some words in Hebrew that sound the same in Japanese but have very different meanings. You then have to build a sentence out of these words. For example, the word *isha*, which in Japanese means *doctor* but in Hebrew means *woman*. Or the word *sakana*, which in Japanese means *fish* but in Hebrew means *danger*."

Mr. Inui listened attentively and appeared to genuinely consider, albeit his slight intoxication, this game as part of his personal entertainment. Then he shoved another dried silver fish into his already full mouth, cracking its head off enthusiastically and looked as if he was doing the math.

I counted in my head, *Three ... two ... one!*

As expected, he turned to me and shouted out, "Sala-san, *isha sakana*!"

Just like clockwork! I told myself, reassuring him with a smile that he was spot-on.

It took a few additional moments before my real intention sank in and, judging by the subtle change in his gaze, he seemed to have gotten the message—*Dangerous Woman*. My smile, and clearly my body language, had him register that our game was over.

I was not the prey that he had anticipated.

By the way, the alternative scenarios had been less friendly, some even involving the unsolicited use of utensils in various unguarded organs!

For now, at least, Mr. Inui seemed drunk enough not to take my rejection too harshly. His sleazy gesture toward the semi-automatic, semi-natural responses of our well-trained waitress appeared to soothe his unmet appetite.

But then, without warning, he suddenly became restless, and finally snapped. He gathered his team and broke up the party.

Wow ... seems everyone is hormonal today!

I looked at him, trying to figure out where that sudden mood change had come from. He looked back at me, and his eyes spelled *disappointment*.

He leaned over in my direction and whispered toward me indiscreetly, "You could have gained another week."

As Mr. Inui walked out, tailed by his tipsy team, Mr. Kobayashi sought my gaze, trying to comprehend what had just happened. I understood his need to know, but I could not get myself to look back at him nor say a word.

Left with no choice, Mr. Kobayashi wrapped things up elegantly and, soon, we were all out the door. He then ordered two cabs, and while he took a cab alone with Tom, he asked me to accompany the rest of the European team back to their hotel. Our remaining team bowed to us genially as we got into the cabs. Then they waved goodbye to us until we turned the corner.

In Tokyo traffic, a five-minute ride took us close to twenty minutes, but the Europeans riding with me seemed happy enough to enjoy the views of Tokyo's colorful nightlife in silence, jet-lagged and drunk enough for a good night's sleep. I was relieved that I didn't need to entertain them, as I already had enough discussions going on in my head. I was not only upset, I felt harassed, which made me furious.

What the hell is wrong with men? Can't any of them control themselves?

And was the Sweaty Swine truly considering blackmailing me? Is he for real? Yuck! I can't believe he had his sweaty hand on me! As if it is not enough that Mr. Inui has forced his way into my dreams. He actually tried to shove a pacifier in my mouth this evening, expecting me to silently surrender?

We arrived at the hotel and found Mr. Kobayashi and Tom already saying their goodbyes in the lobby. Tom bowed nonstop, like a wind-up doll—either he was very drunk or just trying too hard to comply with local manners. Whatever the reason, it was actually quite amusing and, for a moment, I managed to shut out the unwanted recollections of the evening's events and let out a silent laugh. At last, the European team entered the elevator, and Mr. Kobayashi and I waved until the doors shut.

I waited for Mr. Kobayashi to ask me what had happened, but he just turned on his heels and walked out of the hotel without saying a word.

I stood still, hoping he would return, but after waiting long enough to see a few empty elevators fill up, I realized that he was not coming back. It made me feel even more humiliated.

I turned to leave and suddenly noticed Mr. Kobayashi's briefcase laying on the floor where he had been standing. It was not like him to be so careless.

Then another wave of disgust, filled with shame and anger, took over me as I reconstructed in my head the images of Mr. Inui shoving his hand up my thigh. I felt sick to my stomach and ran to the restroom. I pressed the running water soundtrack button on the side of the toilet and hovered over the seat, trying to relieve the queasiness.

I left the cubicle and splashed some cold water on my face, washing off my makeup in the process. Then I quickly fixed myself to look at least a little decent before I entered society again.

I went back to the lobby and found Mr. Kobayashi's briefcase just where he had left it. After some consideration, I decided to both text Mr. Kobayashi and leave a message at the hotel reception, letting him know I had his briefcase. Then I finally called it a day.

When I got back home, I found Ben at the kitchen bar. As soon as he looked at me, he knew something was wrong. He got up and searched my face attentively for hints as to what had happened.

We silently stood across from each other, but I could not bring myself to look him in the eye. A tear ran down my cheek, and Ben opened his arms and approached me silently. I fell into his embrace.

I cried. No place in the world felt to me more secure at the very moment than within Ben's arms. I knew Ben saw me for who I was. I felt protected.

I took his hand and led him to our bedroom, quietly closing the door behind us.

Chapter 20: Making The Call

The next morning, as soon as I arrived at the office, I headed over to Mr. Kobayashi's desk to hand him his briefcase. I was hoping he would be happy to get it back and that this would make up for the undesired and unfortunate incident with Mr. Inui.

But Mr. Kobayashi was not at his desk.

At 10:00 a.m., as scheduled, Mr. Inui and Tom arrived with their teams. I welcomed them all at the reception and accompanied them to the meeting room.

There was still no sign of Mr. Kobayashi.

"I apologize on behalf of Mr. Kobayashi," I opened, exploiting my most confident smile. "He will be joining us shortly." I didn't have the faintest idea where Mr. Kobayashi was nor when, or if, he planned on showing up.

As soon as the OL entered the room with our refreshments, I excused myself and left the meeting room to try Mr. Kobayashi's cell phone once more. There was still no answer.

I showed up at Yuki's desk, dragging him away from Silent Rie. *I really don't trust silent people.*

"I need your help! Mr. Kobayashi hasn't shown up." I continued, devising a plan as I spoke, "I need Tom and Mr. Inui kept entertained and away from the office today; otherwise, we will never get things moving within the week." The words shot out of my mouth before I really knew what my game plan was. "Do you think you could take them to the sumo tournament today? Perhaps get some VIP seats and show them a good time?"

Yuki taking Tom and Mr. Inui to the sumo tournament wouldn't even sound so peculiar, considering Yuki's own sumo past. My thoughts were marathoning through my mind as I spoke.

Yuki fixed me with a curious but unquestioning look, grabbed his cell phone, and then went out through the glass doors to make some calls. Meanwhile, I tried calling Mr. Kobayashi again. Still no answer.

As I walked back to the meeting room, wondering how to buy more time, Yuki caught up with me, a broad smile on his face, his eyes signaling victory. Not only had he gotten them VIP seats, but he had also persuaded two of his old sumo pals to hold up bogus sponsorship signs for both automotive companies. Clearly, we had neither the budget nor the authority to actually pay for their sponsorships, but his buddies were happy to show their loyalty to a friend in need and overlook that minor detail.

"So, you really were a sumo star! It's not just a pick-up line!" I smiled at him as we entered the meeting room together.

"Okay, it is settled," I announced, drawing everyone's attention my way in an instant.

"Yuki will be taking the heads of the two negotiating teams to the sumo tournament today, as Mr. Kobayashi has arranged VIP seats."

The room was silent with anticipation.

"In order to show our deep appreciation for all the work that has been put into this merger so far, and to welcome Mr. Weber properly, we have also decided to purchase sponsorships in the names of both your companies." I bowed my head slightly, hoping I was finally out of harm's way.

"It is a great honor to be sponsoring the Tokyo Grand Sumo Tournament." Surprisingly, Mr. Inui took the bait without further questions, showing unexpected spontaneity. Then he smiled at Tom, trying to impress on Tom the magnitude of the gesture.

"And Mr. Kobayashi will be meeting us there?" Tom added, faint concern in his voice.

"Of course!" I reassured him with a bright smile. "Mr. Kobayashi apologizes profusely for not being here this morning, but we thought you would both appreciate our little surprise. And while you enjoy the tournament, I will go through the details of our updated analyses with your teams so that you can both receive full reports tomorrow morning."

I accompanied Yuki and the two men to the elevator and waved to them until the doors closed. Then I took in some air, feeling it had become thinner since they had arrived.

I tried Mr. Kobayashi's cell phone once more. This time, I left a message, which I hoped didn't sound too desperate yet projected enough urgency.

Loosening the bun in my hair, I returned to the meeting room. *You can do it!* I told myself.

"Let's start with the figures," I dove right in, aware that the members of both parties were still unsure whether to comply. "From our latest analyses, we have seen that, by merging the weaker segments of both companies, our synergy could potentially grow the combined business revenues by ten to fifteen percent in the first year and fifteen to twenty percent over the next two consecutive years …"

Very soon, everyone was engaged in discussion, raising suggestions, offering scenarios, and all in good faith. In Japan, as long as there was true willingness to do business, the million dollar formula was simple: keep justifications logical, systematic, and moral, and progress is more likely than not.

Throughout the day, Yuki kept messaging me amusing texts and photos. The three of them were clearly having a good time. I, on the other hand, battled hard to keep it together as I left the meeting room at every given opportunity in an attempt to reach Mr. Kobayashi on his cell phone.

Every few hours, Yuki texted me to say that Mr. Inui and Tom were asking about Mr. Kobayashi, and I replied that he should either continue making excuses or get them too drunk to care. Yuki seemed to find my second suggestion more practical. And so, by the time the tournament was over, I received photos on my cell phone with both Tom and Mr. Inui in odd, uncensored poses, wearing *mawashi*, the sumo wrestlers' underwear-like traditional attire. Then, in the next set of photos, both Mr. Inui and Tom were passed out in the back seat of the taxi; Tom's head on Mr. Inui's shoulder.

How cute! I texted Yuki, trying to restrain my laughter in front of the vastly progressing and hard-working professional teams.

By the end of the day, the negotiating teams had a dozen detailed scenarios worked out, all backed up by the winning formula—logical, systematic, and moral—and we were ready to present them to the heads of the teams. I presented the closing summary for the day, and Mr. Koga, the most senior member of Mr. Inui's group, suggested we all go out for dinner. This was the final stamp of approval that at least the teams were moving forward nicely.

As we approached the elevators, I gently but assertively made my excuses and wished them all a wonderful evening. I could not get away with another day of Mr. Kobayashi's absence, and so I needed to figure out my options. It was already only sheer luck that none of our superiors had asked for him all day.

A few minutes after the teams left, Yuki called to tell me that our VIPs had both been safely delivered to their hotels.

"To make sure they both passed out for the rest of the evening, we finished the day with a round of drinks at a topless bar, and then a short stop at a place I would rather not name," Yuki concluded his report, sounding quite happy with the outcome.

"I have heard enough," I quickly replied with unspoken approval for any further details regarding their adventure. "You are my hero," I added before we ended our call.

It was nearly 8:00 p.m., and I assumed I was the only one left on our office floor. It was so unlike Mr. Kobayashi to disappear like that. I kept telling myself, *Unless ... Well, unless something has happened to him.* I quickly hushed that disturbing thought and tried his cell phone once more, but this time I actually heard it ring. *What the hell?* I quickly turned my eyes in the direction of his desk.

Oh my God!

I got up from my seat and raced to it, but Mr. Kobayashi was not there and his briefcase was just as I had left it this morning. *That can't be possible. I know I heard his cell phone ringing!* I redialed, and the phone rang out loud again. *Oh no!* I looked down and realized that Mr. Kobayashi's cell phone was in his briefcase.

I picked up the briefcase, laying it on the desk with mounting concern. For a moment, I felt dizzy, realizing things might even be worse than I had imagined.

What if Mr. Kobayashi had wanted his briefcase to be found and left a note inside? Should I take a look? If so, should I be the first to read it?

I stepped closer to the briefcase and, just as I was about to open it, my hands began to tremble. *Maybe Mr. Kobayashi left the briefcase on purpose for me to find, and now I have wasted a whole day and he can no longer be saved.*

No, there is probably a perfectly good explanation.

I tried to calm myself. I ran my hands over the buckle a number of times, but I couldn't quite bring myself to make the move.

It feels so unethical to go through his personal belongings, I told myself, gathering the strength to move forward.

Just then, his cell phone rang again. *This time it isn't me calling! Maybe it is Mr. Kobayashi himself. This phone call might lead me to him!*

I looked at the briefcase, and just as I had gathered the courage to open the buckle and snatch his cell phone out, the ringing stopped.

His wife! Oh no. Now what? Should I call her back? What will I tell her? She obviously called him because he is not with her ...

What if he is with Ms. Perfect, the drama star?

I stood there, holding his cell phone, then finally put it back in the briefcase.

Just as I was about to close the briefcase, something familiar caught my eye from underneath a pile of paperwork. Unable to resist, I lifted the paperwork up just enough to see that it was a copy of my favorite Japanese fashion magazine. I had been so busy lately that I hadn't even had the time to peek at its cover in the convenience store. *How bad would it be if I just took a quick look through it? It would be just like going through the magazine at a newsstand, right?*

Still, just knowing that Mr. Kobayashi carries a copy of it in his briefcase kind of sheds a whole new light on his personality, which he would probably prefer to keep private. Unless, of course, he got it for his wife before he was abducted by aliens or, more likely, the Yakuza and never got to give it to her ... Well, a tiny peek can't hurt ...

I carefully removed the magazine from underneath the pile of papers. *Okay! Cover photo: Ms. Perfect. That explains why he has it in his briefcase!*

Her photo upset me, as it made me think about how unfaithful men could be.

I slipped the magazine back into the briefcase then quickly covered it with the paperwork. I buckled up the briefcase, put it back on the floor next to Mr. Kobayashi's desk, and then left the office. I was so overwhelmed by the past two days that I decided to let go of it all and just pray that Mr. Kobayashi showed up to work tomorrow.

When I finally got home, I found Ben asleep in our bed. At first, I was bothered by his swift relocation from the sofa, but before I could even give it another thought, I passed out on the bed beside him.

Chapter 21: A Pink Note

"A pink note! You're kidding me, right?" I snapped at the innocent and already apologetic subway conductor who was simply doing his job.

Delays in public transportation were very rare in Japan; therefore, when such a delay did occur, subway officials handed pink notes out to the passengers, taking responsibility for their delay. Funny thing was, without a pink note, people were more likely to believe the dog ate your homework than that public transportation had actually come in late.

Murphy's Law had made it to my bed this morning and seemed to be trailing me to the office, as well. First, I had woken up late because my cell phone battery had run out, so the alarm hadn't gone off. Then I'd had to run to catch the subway, but even the staff, whose job it was to push passengers from the platform and onto the train, had fallen short in finding a spot to fit me in. And now, just when I was finally three hundred feet away from my station, ready to make a run for it, the train had come to a halt, the lights had dimmed, and the conductor had announced this unexpected delay.

I don't even know whether my boss is still alive, let alone whether I still have a job, considering I was meant to present yesterday's joint team findings twenty-seven minutes ago. On any normal day, I would have been quite amused to receive a legendary pink note, but today of all days!

It was 9:52 a.m. when I entered the office, sweating like the Sweaty Swine's wife and as pink as the note in my purse. I was nearly an hour late.

As I got closer to the meeting room, I realized I might be in more trouble than I'd anticipated. Not only was my boss, Mr. Kobayashi, still absent, but his boss, Mr. Hashimoto, was sitting at the head of the table, talking with the teams! *Now what?* I asked myself, still trying to catch my breath. I felt a bit dizzy.

I had never spoken to Mr. Hashimoto. I wouldn't even know how to approach him. Should I introduce myself? What if they had told him about the firm's alleged sponsoring of the sumo tournament in their names? What if Mr. Hashimoto was furious with me for not telling him about Mr. Kobayashi's disappearance? What if he thought I had gone behind Mr. Kobayashi's back and broke the codes of hierarchy, and now I was, therefore, no longer fit to work for a Japanese firm?

My hand slipped into my bag, searching for the pink note and hoping that it might cut me some slack.

Just as I was about to open the door, Yuki showed up behind me and pulled me aside.

"What is it? You scared the hell out of me!" I glared at him impatiently.

"I thought you would like to know that the actress, Hiroko-san, the one from the TV drama series, dropped by

Mr. Hashimoto's office this morning," Yuki started off, and I stared at him, hoping to hear some useful news. "When she left, Mr. Hashimoto told us that Mr. Kobayashi will be absent for the next few weeks," he added.

I tried to put two and two together, but nothing made sense.

"Is that it?" I asked, still impatient, although I was thankful that Yuki had thought to fill me in on that.

Yuki nodded.

I thanked him to show my appreciation for the information then turned back to the meeting room, cautiously opening the door.

As soon as Tom saw me, the oddest thing happened. He stood, applauding with admiration.

Who is he applauding? I asked myself and turned around, fully expecting to find Mr. Kobayashi standing behind me. No one was there.

Everyone else in the room then got up and joined Tom's applause.

I remained rooted to the spot, speechless.

"The teams have just concluded their presentation, and we are all very excited about the scenarios you propose," Tom declared.

I scanned the room carefully, but it seemed that everyone, including Mr. Inui, was in tune with Tom.

"I have recommended that we meet again to conclude things when Mr. Kobayashi returns," Mr. Inui added.

I warily took a seat, trying to figure out quite how my luck had turned.

Thirty minutes later, I was still witnessing the miracle.

Everything seemed to be going surprisingly well!

Mr. Hashimoto finally wrapped up the meeting, thanked both teams for their readiness to move forward, and wished everyone the best of luck.

As soon as the elevator doors closed and the teams were gone, Mr. Hashimoto turned to me and said, "Sala-san, please get your purse. You're coming with me."

I bowed politely then headed back to the meeting room, my thoughts starting to haranguing me from within. Was he sending me home? Now I was probably going to pay for my presumptuousness or, as the Japanese saying went, "the nail sticking out will be hammered into place."

I had to admit that I had gone a bit beyond my station as a Key Account Analyst … but what choice had I had? I had to do what I had to do! I could have gone to Mr. Hashimoto yesterday and notified him of Mr. Kobayashi's absence, but then we would have probably lost our chance with Mr. Inui. On the other hand, maybe Mr. Hashimoto had sold me off as one of Mr. Inui's slaves, and he just wanted to fill me in … Or maybe he needed me to help convince Mr. Kobayashi to leave Ms. Perfect and come back down to reality. *Okay, that sounds more like it.*

Mr. Hashimoto and I climbed into one of the company cars, and the driver shut the door behind us. I had no idea where we were going, and I had a feeling I might not like where he was taking me.

The ride was long, and the farther we got from the office, the more anxious I became.

"I have a pink note from the subway," I finally blurted out, trying to break the unbearable silence.

Mr. Hashimoto nodded just enough for me to see that he had heard me.

I immediately regretted having said that, but I had never really learned the Japanese way of not talking if you had nothing good to say.

Please say something, I found myself begging Mr. Hashimoto in my head as my mind filled with images of me not tolerating the silence any longer and falling into despair performing hara-kiri. But then the car made a sharp turn, and we entered the gates of a hospital.

"Our clients are happy. I will tell Mr. Kobayashi you did a good job, Sala-san," Mr. Hashimoto suddenly remarked.

"Oh no. Is Mr. Kobayashi in the hospital?" I asked, realizing that option had never crossed my mind. Then I grasped the huge compliment I had just been paid.

"Yes," answered Mr. Hashimoto, stepping out of the car and waiting for me to follow. As we entered the hospital, he continued, "On Wednesday night, Mr. Kobayashi was found unconscious outside the hotel where the European team is staying. The only thing they found on him was Hiroko-san's business card, which was tucked into his pocket. She had visited him in the office that same morning and, luckily, she had given him her card. They found it last night, and she came to inform me today that Mr. Kobayashi is hospitalized here."

The image of Mr. Kobayashi's briefcase, cell phone, and the magazine with Ms. Perfect on its cover flashed before my eyes, but I quickly conclude they were irrelevant. The fact that Mr. Kobayashi had been found unconscious on the night that Mr. Inui had walked out so abruptly on our small dinner party made me feel somewhat guilty.

As we headed down the main corridor, Hiroko-san was walking in our direction. *She is as pretty in person as she is on the cover of the magazine*, I thought to myself as she got closer.

She is stunning.

She exchanged a few polite words with Mr. Hashimoto before turning my way and extending her hand for a handshake. *Oh, one of those. I haven't shaken a Japanese hand for quite a while.*

I offered her my hand, fully expecting a dead fish handshake. But no, she was possibly the first Japanese woman who I had encountered to actually get the handshake right. She was not afraid to argue, seemed to speak her mind, and knew how to shake hands properly. We could actually be friends.

Hiroko-san led us to Mr. Kobayashi's room where we found him pale-faced, lying silently in an impeccably made-up bed, connected to various machines.

Mr. Hashimoto exchanged a few words at the door with a nurse who had just attended to Mr. Kobayashi. The nurse then excused herself, exiting apologetically as we walked in.

Next thing I knew, Mr. Hashimoto turned my way and said, "Sala-san, please notify me of any changes in Mr. Kobayashi's condition." He then bowed and thanked Ms. Perfect again for caring for Mr. Kobayashi and excused himself.

I nodded quietly as he left, still in shock, trying to make sense out of the chain of events over the past few days. I took a seat next to Hiroko-san as Mr. Hashimoto closed the door behind him.

"I broke his heart," Hiroko-san confessed in a cracked

voice after a few moments of silence. I could sense the sincerity of her feelings for him.

"I'm sure it wasn't your fault," I answered, assuming, however, that their incident must have greatly influenced his condition, not helped, of course, by my own modest contribution that same evening.

We sat for a while, not saying a word, until the door opened and a nurse walked in again. It took me another moment before I noticed Mr. Kobayashi's wife standing behind her. Hiroko-san and I got up and bowed to Mrs. Kobayashi, offering the appropriate greetings. Then the nurse left the room and Mrs. Kobayashi sat down next to me.

Okay, this is definitely a soap opera now!

I tried to understand quite how both women could sit there in total silence, exchanging neither a word nor a glimpse, just being there for the man who they both seemed to really care for. Then Mrs. Kobayashi broke the silence with a soft but shattered voice.

"Sala-san, do you know what *karoshi* means?"

I nodded politely. *Karoshi* is the Japanese term for someone dying as a result of overworking. I wondered whether Mrs. Kobayashi was remorseful for not stopping her husband from overworking.

The three of us sat there silently, each nursing her own pile of guilt.

In the midst of this dead silence and without warning, Mr. Kobayashi mumbled something. All three of us jumped to our feet and approached his bed. At first, we could not make out what he was saying, but as he kept repeating one word, it slowly became clear.

Finally, his wife said, "He is calling out the name of a woman. Someone by the name of Kumiko."

"Maybe Kumiko is one of the nurses," I replied with a sincere hope that there wasn't a third woman to throw into this already complex drama.

"Maybe," Mrs. Kobayashi answered with a hopeful smile.

"I'll go and ask," I said, trying to keep her spirits up.

Just as I was about to leave the room, Hiroko-san announced, "Kumiko was my mother's name. He is calling out for her."

Mrs. Kobayashi and I turned and stared at her in shock.

Before we could say another word, Hiroko-san covered her mouth, burst into tears, grabbed her coat, and then ran out.

I stood still for another moment, trying to understand what had just happened, and then I walked out into the hallway to find her, but she was gone.

I went back to the room to find Mrs. Kobayashi sitting beside her husband, crying. I quietly reached for my bag and coat to leave, hopeful they both survived this drama.

Chapter 22: Confessions And Angels

The image of Mrs. Kobayashi crying beside her husband's bed stayed with me all day, like a shadow. The only fact that comforted me was that weekend had begun and I could hopefully manage to get some rest.

Every morning this week, I had visited Mr. Kobayashi before going to the office and reporting to Mr. Hashimoto. Today was the first time I arrived at the hospital to find him alone, without visitors, sitting in bed and staring out the window.

He had made great progress since last Friday. Luckily, he had only had a mild heart attack, and it was the fall that had caused most of the damage. He had a few broken ribs and had suffered a concussion. I was relieved. Although, considering his entanglement with two, if not three, different women, I couldn't help thinking that his troubles had only just begun.

The way he was looking out the window reminded me of the day when I had watched him gaze out from behind his desk after Hiroko-san had stormed out of our office.

I sat and tried not to intrude on his private moment.

Eventually, he turned to me and greeted me with unusual

warmth in his eyes. "Sala-san, thank you. You did a good job. Mr. Hashimoto was very happy."

"Oh no, no, I did nothing." I took on the common, self-effacing Japanese response, although I had to admit that it was a relief to hear some praise from him. I also had no doubt that, considering the cards I had in hand, I did seem to have won this poker round quite brilliantly, against all odds.

After a long pause and endless debates in my head, I finally gave in. "Mr. Kobayashi, I have a small question." I hesitated a moment more but finally plucked up the courage to ask, "Do you know anyone by the name of Kumiko?"

Mr. Kobayashi seemed rather taken aback by my question, but after I recounted that he had muttered her name several times in front of Hiroko-san and his wife, he eventually replied, "Kumiko was my wife."

"You were married before?"

"Yes. Many years ago, when I was very young."

"So, Hiroko-san is your—"

"Yes, my daughter," he responded before I could finish the sentence.

I was dumbstruck. "So, why did Hiroko-san say she broke your heart? And what about her mother, your first wife? Where is she?" I asked, immediately regretting my inappropriateness and recalling that personal conversations with him were off limit.

After weighing his words, Mr. Kobayashi answered, "When Hiroko was five years old, Kumiko killed herself."

I stayed silent, not sure what I should say, but since I lacked the ability of simply not saying anything, I finally added, "I am sorry," while scanning his eyes, but I saw nothing but an empty gaze.

For a moment, I froze in place, considering how to retreat from a discussion that seemed to have become way too personal for Mr. Kobayashi's weak heart to carry.

"After she died," Mr. Kobayashi suddenly started, "I could not face Hiroko and was not in any shape to raise her alone, so I moved to Tokyo to start a new life. Kumiko's mother raised Hiroko. She told Hiroko we had both died in a car crash. Hiroko was just a young child," he whispered, trying to stop himself from breaking into tears, though I could feel the heavy burden of his sadness.

"Wow," I responded, still cautious yet intrigued by Mr. Kobayashi's new persona slowly building in my mind.

We remained silent for a while.

"Last month, Kumiko's mother died, and Hiroko discovered the truth." I saw a tear roll down his cheek, and I began to tear up, as well. "She came to my office to … to ask me to collect her mother's ashes," he finally added and could no longer hold it, breaking into a painful cry. "She is angry. She says she wants nothing to do with her past and that I may as well be dead."

Mr. Kobayashi lay back down on his bed and closed his eyes, trying to gather himself quietly.

The image of Hiroko-san running off, crying as he called out her mother's name, appears before my eyes, and I feel genuine sympathy for her. I couldn't start to imagine what she was going through, her personal telenovela even more complex than the one she played on TV.

Before I left the room, I turned to Mr. Kobayashi one last time, unable to fully let go of the subject. "Tell your daughter that you are proud of the strong woman she has become. Tell her you never stopped loving her, for all it is worth. That is what I would want my father to say." I retreated slowly then, quietly shutting the door behind me.

After returning to the office to update Mr. Hashimoto, I closed some loose ends at the office then went home, anticipating an early night.

As I walked through the front door to our apartment, the TV in our bedroom was exceptionally loud. I had been on edge since my visit at the hospital in the morning and simply could not add any additional noise to that already going on inside my head. So, I went into the bedroom, irritated, just to shut the noise off, and found Ben on the floor, his back to the bed, head hanging down and a whiskey bottle in his hand.

I knelt down and carefully, unwillingly lifted Ben's head. I felt as if I would simply break into pieces if the world did not send me some super powers.

"I can't!" I cried out. Then I forced myself to come close enough to check if he was breathing. *He is breathing.*

I frantically got up and turned off the TV, feeling as if the room was getting smaller and smaller every second. Tears were gushing out without control as I stared at the darkened TV for a while, trying to catch my breath and eventually collect myself.

I realized my night had just begun.

I got a bucket then sat on the floor next to Ben.

"Why, Ben?" I whispered at him, knowing he couldn't hear me anyway.

I looked at him, unable to find any more empathy for him. I tried to get him to throw up, but he just put his head on my knees. I pushed his head up again and again toward the bucket, frustrated and angry. His head was heavy and simply fell back onto my knees every time I tried. *I can't believe this is happening. Again!*

A few years ago, we had been on holiday in Amsterdam and had met this really nice couple who had invited us to a costume party at their home in Berlin.

Germany had always been a taboo for Ben and his family, due to his grandparents' history, so he had sworn me to keep this little detour to ourselves.

We had bought costumes at a secondhand shop in Amsterdam. Ben had chosen a devil costume with red devil horns and a pointy red tail. I had gone for pajamas and a nightcap.

When we had arrived at the party, a militant-looking woman, dressed as an angel and wearing black lipstick and black nail polish, opened the door for us. Thrilled by the devil counterpart standing in front of her, she had grabbed Ben's hand—graciously ignoring me—and had led him to the kitchen. Ben had seemed happy, so I'd walked out to the tiny porch and had been quickly drawn into a deep conversation with a gay German couple dressed up as a camel, each with a hump on his head.

"Something has happened to Ben!" had been the five words that the angel had repeated as she had rushed me into the kitchen.

I had found Ben sitting near the center table, his head tilted and white foam coming out of his mouth. At first, I had been stupefied—I had never seen him in such a state. The last thing I could handle was Ben being taken to a hospital in

Germany, of all places, and us having to keep this secret to ourselves for the rest of our lives. And of course, if he were to be hospitalized, would I not be able to tell his parents since I had been sworn to secrecy about us being in Germany in the first place?

Luckily, the gay-camel couple had been more experienced than me. They had brought a bucket and dragged Ben to the floor, encouraging him to throw up. But, just as now, Ben had put his head on my knees and had fallen asleep.

"He will be fine. Just keep checking that he is still breathing," they had calmly advised.

I had ended up sitting on guard, confused and anxious all night, checking his breathing frantically every few minutes.

The next morning, Ben had had no recollection of passing out. I, on the other hand, had never forgotten how helpless I had felt. And now, here we were again, his head on my knees, the bucket at our sides.

I spent another restless night, constantly checking that he was still breathing, helplessly alone.

"We need to go our separate ways," was the first thing I said when Ben opened his eyes and I could see he had regained consciousness. I had been waiting all night to say those words, and I didn't want to even hear him explain. I was never more certain of anything in my life.

I'm done.

Chapter 23: Closure

After that last drinking episode, it took Ben and me less than three months to sever what was left of our bond. When I had told Ben I thought it was best for us to go our separate ways, he had seemed surprisingly relieved. Perhaps he had realized that it was time to find his own dream and not continue living miserably through my Japanese fantasy. He had decided to go back to the US and had, apparently, started writing his fifth novel, this one about an American businesswoman living in Japan.

"It is physically painful to leave, you know?" he had said to me with a sad, candid smile before boarding the express train to Narita Airport.

I had hugged him tightly, trying to be strong for the both of us.

"I feel as if I've lost part of me," he had then whispered, detaching himself to board the train.

My eyes had boarded the train with him, and just as Ben had turned back to say something, the doors had closed, shutting me out of his life for good.

I knew exactly what Ben had meant when he'd said it

was "physically painful." We were like Siamese twins connected from our waists to our shoulders and torn apart against our nature.

It was clear to us both that, even after he had gotten on that train, we would remain wounded, needing time to heal. We hadn't break up from lack of love; we had broken up from lack of life. We had been depriving each other of oxygen, and in order to have a fulfilling life, we needed to part and relearn how to survive on our own.

I decided to stay in our apartment. Some days, I felt sad going back to an empty home, but most of the time, I was actually relieved. Now that I could conserve all my energy for myself, I felt revitalized. I was free to be happy and spontaneous, to laugh, wear sneakers, and meet with blacklisted friends. Well, that part didn't happen so often. I guessed that was part of moving on, as well.

Rachel and I had only spoken once since Ben and I had broken up. She had called to tell me that she and Noah had twin girls.

Working hard to close the automotive deal also helped to keep my spirits up. When Mr. Kobayashi returned from his sick leave, there were still some ups and downs in finalizing the contract, but the general attitude was positive. A sense of true will and harmony led both parties to succeed and provided Mr. Inui with the confidence that he needed in order to believe that the Europeans had finally understood the Japanese spirit. Both parties wanted to make it happen, and it finally had.

There was, it would seem, something else that kept Tom excited about closing the deal, aside from his concerns about raging Japanese spirits, thumb-chopping Yakuza, and the good of his corporation. He had a personal agenda.

Sometime after the unspoken sumo adventure, Yuki had revealed that he and Tom had hit it off and were working on a little personal merger of their own. Tom's subsequent relocation to Japan, more specifically to Yuki's apartment, seemed like a gratifying bonus with which to close the deal. Yuki's confession reassured me that he saw me as much as a friend as I saw him, and that made me all the happier.

Soon after the deal was closed, I was promoted to division manager, becoming the first woman and the first foreigner to have been offered an executive position since the firm had been founded. I replaced Mr. Kobayashi, who was given a special titular consulting position and remained unofficially my superior. Mr. Hashimoto was behind this transition and had made it very smooth. It was clear that Mr. Kobayashi had enough to deal with and, most of all, needed to reduce his workload and take better care of his health. He accepted his new status with gratitude, aware that the most important merger of his life was still ahead of him—the union of his now extended family.

As to my personal life, whenever Mrs. Toda and I crossed paths, she invited me to move into "Sala's Room." She insisted that, "It is not good for a woman to live alone."

Truth be told, I wasn't sure whether she was referring to me or to herself. However, as reassuring as it would be to have a mother figure around, I still felt I had things I needed to figure out on my own.

Chapter 24: When Life Takes A Turn

A blast of fresh air hit me in the chest as he stepped into the South Wing Executive Lounge. Although men often looked good in business suits, he looked like the symbol of power itself. His strong features were not suppressed by the European outfit of conformity, but rather looked down on it, suggesting perhaps that what really counted lied underneath. There was something Chilean, almost Indian about him.

His eyes were an earthy, warm brown, his skin as smooth as silk, and his lips wide and luscious. The creases on either side of his eyes told of dark, painful times, which he dared not remember. I was drawn to him as if I was meant to contain him and set him free of his past while allowing him to sow in me the seeds of a better future.

I waited for his approach, a move, even a stare that would make everything around me dissolve into an ocean lacking its tide and thirsting to be filled up. I could not breathe deeply when he was out of sight nor could I breathe lightly when he was in sight.

He watched me, silently stalking me as a lion stalked its prey. It did not take long. I could feel my knees weaken, the noises around me grew, and heat colored my cheeks. My lips were parched, aching for his soft, soothing tongue.

Shit, it's time! I caught a glimpse of the clock above the refreshments and snacks bar and forced myself out of the fantasy world and into common reality. It was not easy to detach my eyes from him, but I told myself that it was simply to save myself from getting lost among his lustful thoughts.

I have to get back to Japan! There are too many Latino men in Europe, I told myself as I tried to subdue the overwhelming noise in my head that was getting more pornographic by the second. I pulled myself together to finally leave the executive lounge.

For the past three weeks, I had been fixating on Latino men, one after the other, in the executive lounge of every single airport I had passed through. I had enough pornographic images in my head to write a best-selling erotica novel.

I seized my bag and left the lounge for the departure gates. As I took a seat at our gate on a cold, metallic bench, I restructured myself and cooled off after nearly dissolving within my fantasies. I checked the time again and realized that Mr. Kobayashi had been souvenir shopping for over two hours.

He had become very sentimental since his heart attack last year, and while I was possessed by Latino men, he went on a shopping frenzy at every single airport. He, too, seemed more alive than ever. In fact, something incredible had happened to him since he and Hiroko-san had finally reunited. Funny thing, he bragged about her incessantly, brazenly breaking the Japanese code of modesty, as if he took on the customary behavior of a "Good Jewish father." Well, I might have had a thing or two to do with that.

On his desk, he had a photo of him walking Hiroko-san down the aisle. Yes, she had tied the knot in probably one of the more publicized and talked about weddings in Japan, her popularity not lagging much behind that of the Imperial House of Japan.

Last month, she had given birth to the cutest baby girl, who had certainly stolen Mr. Kobayashi's heart together with the hearts of most of the Japanese nation.

"Sala-san, our plane …"

I suddenly noticed Mr. Kobayashi standing in front of me with two bags stuffed full of gifts and a baseball cap on his head with the Real Madrid logo on it.

I got up from the bench and joined him to board the flight.

As we took our seats, I felt a sense of relief. Just two more stops to go and our three-week voyage across Europe would finally come to an end. However, this flight took on an undesired turn.

This was, in fact, *the* flight, in which, Mr. Kobayashi passed out after drinking. The flight, in which, I almost reached out for the ice cube that had channeled its way to his crotch. The flight where I grabbed Mr. Kobayashi's hand, though I had never touched him before. The flight when I realized, as the plane dove into total darkness, that I actually had no one out there who really needed me. This was the flight where I unbuckled my seat belt, stood, despite the chaos around me, and yelled at the top of my voice, "I want a baby!"

Chapter 25: Seeking Refuge

On the news, they called it a "crash landing."

At first, the combination of those two words made no sense to me. *How could we have both crashed and landed?* Only after translating my actual experience, feeling the pain of dying yet being spared, did the joining of those words begin to make sense. I have personally both crashed and landed.

Most of the passengers survived the crash, and Mr. Kobayashi and I were relatively spared with only some minor injuries. However, we were both put under surveillance at the Rome/American hospital, obviously in Rome.

The following few nights, I hardly sleep a wink. What haunts me more than anything is the thought that, during those moments, with immense pressure racing through my ears and eyes, not a single person, who genuinely needs me, came to mind.

Even Ben no longer needs me.

The realization of how much I need to be needed is stronger than any feeling I've ever experienced.

When Ben and I had first met, we both agreed that having children was not at the top of our priorities. I had been fully engaged in building my career, and Ben had been trying to figure out how to write his first novel. As I spent many weeks away on business trips, we got into the habit of compensating ourselves with long, pampering weekends at luxury hotels, fancy spas, and exotic nature tours. At the time, this type of lifestyle seemed more attractive than the alternative of changing diapers sixteen times per baby on an average weekend. We thoroughly enjoyed these getaways, and they always seemed to bring out the best in us.

I kept all deeper thoughts of motherhood, therefore, shoved as far away as I possibly could. I wanted to believe that, by making Ben and myself happy and providing for us, I would fulfill my quota of being needed by someone.

Once released from the hospital, we are transferred back to Japan with the white glove service only the Japanese can offer, and I see to it that I am drugged enough to simply glide onto another flight.

Arriving at my apartment, I feel displaced and restless. It is too hard to let go and move on, especially now that I am so conscious of my solitude.

A week later, early Saturday morning, I show up at Mrs. Toda's gate. She is sweeping the pebbled path when she notices me standing there, a suitcase at my feet and bags under my eyes.

"Sala-san!" she calls out.

I raise my eyes from the ground, unable to utter a word.

Mrs. Toda pushes the gate open and places her small, soft hand at the center of my back. She silently leads me through the gate and up the deck toward the temple.

I remove my sneakers, put on the slippers she hands me,

and drag my suitcase behind me, following her down the long, wooden corridor. She opens the door to that very same room where she once sheltered me and my carpet on that miserable, rainy Saturday morning.

The carpet is still there, just where I left it, despite the fact that nearly four years have passed. It's as if she knew I would return, or she simply laid it out that morning, expecting me with her unmatched ability to communicate with me beyond words.

She places a futon on my furry carpet, spreads some linens over it, and then quietly exits the room after setting a pot of tea for me on the small knee-high table in the corner of the room.

For most of the weekend, for the first time since the crash, I sleep like a baby. I somehow find peace in Mrs. Toda's traditional, simplistic home. It connects me to a side of Japan I once loved and lost.

I expect to only stay for a few days, and although I would never impose myself on anyone, I feel that things are different with Mrs. Toda. Then, somehow, the days become weeks, and Mrs. Toda never asks any whys; she simply smiles and reassures me in a subtle but heartfelt way that everything is fine, that I am welcomed to stay for as long as I want. I accept the motherly protection I have been longing for, even though it is such an odd feeling knowing that she had the intuition that I would be back.

Flashbacks of the crash landing visit me in my dreams, some nights waking me up in deep anxiety. Everything in my life seems chaotic, and for the first time in many years, I feel I don't have it "all figured out." I am shocked by how overwhelmed I am for wanting the most natural thing a woman could desire—a baby.

Being a recently divorced, workaholic alien living in a Buddhist temple in the center of Tokyo with no social life whatsoever, I don't really feel on the right path for having a baby.

I am terrified that maybe I have done it all wrong by not aspiring to the American Dream with the loving husband, two kids, a dog, and a house in the suburbs. I never imagined that I would be so confused about the only life I have ever really wanted—the one I have here in Japan. The more I think about it, the more confused I become.

It's not as if I have any alternatives set up. This is the life I know, and the life I have created for myself.

Some nights, I step up to the front deck of the temple with Dharma following me, and I hold him quietly in my arms, yearning to feel how it would be to hold a baby. I close my eyes and feel its heartbeat between my chest and my arm, until I am ready go back to bed, in a more peaceful mode.

In the meantime, Mrs. Toda greets me every morning at the low dining table with breakfast. As I take my seat, she places a tray in front of me laden with miso soup, a bowl of rice, raw eggs, and *umeboshi*—Japanese pickled plums. She sits across from me in silence, and whenever our eyes meet, she smiles at me, and I smile back.

As a coffee-and-biscuit-on-the-run type of person, miso soup and raw eggs for breakfast has taken some getting used to, but I surrender to it and, before long, I find myself oddly but truly enjoying it.

Chapter 26: Numbers And Whisky

During my second weekend at the temple, I meet Akira, a graceful monk and loyal disciple of Mrs. Toda's late husband. After some basic greetings, Akira offers a sympathetic bow and a friendly smile before leaving to chant sutras at the family altar. Apparently, since the death of Mrs. Toda's husband, he comes every day at noon, chants at the family altar, and meditates in the main temple hall.

I return to the office two weeks after my return to Japan. There, I function effortlessly, like a robot programmed for the task. On the evenings when I get back at a reasonable hour, I sit on the deck of the temple and relax, listening to Mrs. Toda practice her karaoke. After long days at the office, clients, bosses, dinners, presentations, meeting rooms, and identical slippers, the open air and simplicity of life with Mrs. Toda, the singing widow of a Buddhist Priest, makes me feel profoundly tranquil.

I have kept things moving forward and have brought in several new clients. I was even asked, for the first time, to present the division's quarterly results at the upcoming board meeting.

Aside from Yuki, no one has the slightest idea that I seek refuge in a Buddhist temple on a fluffy white carpet with a white Persian cat.

Today is the big day, and as I enter the meeting room on the floor above our office, I feel a bit nervous. The grey-suited executives with expressionless faces and identical slippers assemble around the long, shiny wooden table, all ready to note my numbers. It is the first time I have been asked to do this, as it was always Mr. Kobayashi's job. Yet, since he returned to Japan after the crash landing incident, he has not really come back to work. He's on leave without an explicit day for his return, at least none that he shares with me. He called me last night to wish me good luck and told me how his granddaughter has just started smiling. I'm happy he is able to enjoy these moments.

The meeting ends, and as the men collect their belongings, I look around the room and conclude that it went well. I remain last in the meeting room, thanking everyone for attending, and just as I turn to leave, the OL walks in.

"Mr. Hashimoto has asked to see you in his office," she says in her soft, polite voice.

I raise my eyes, surprised.

She apologizes for the intrusion then returns back to her desk.

I haven't spoken to Mr. Hashimoto in person since Mr. Kobayashi was released from the hospital. I hope Mr. Kobayashi is okay and that Mr. Hashimoto's calling me to his office has nothing to do with him this time. In my presentation, I followed the scenario formula with precision, and my numbers appeared to satisfy him, so I can't imagine that would have to do with it.

It would have been nice to come to a meeting with him a bit more prepared ...

"Sala-san. *Dozo*," Mr. Hashimoto says from within his office as I approach his door, inviting me in while pointing to a black leather chair across from his seat on the other side of the table.

I sit down on the edge of my chair, hands on knees, like any polite Japanese woman, trying my best not to look too tense.

He closes the door then puts a bottle of Suntory whisky on the table in front of me. I immediately understand ... *It can't be good news.*

He pours us both a respectable amount for a mid-day, off-the-record whiskey, raises his glass and, with a kind smile, says, "*Kampai*."

"*Kampai*," I answer, adding the obligatory "*itadakimasu*," as expected, thanking him for the drink. I am intrigued yet revisit the thought that this can't be good news.

He waits for me to finish the first round before pouring a second.

"Sala-san, you are one of our best," the unexpected suddenly shoots out of him.

I am not sure how to respond. Such a forthright compliment from someone so senior in the organization is not something I am familiar with in the Japanese corporate context.

I run some possible storylines through my mind but just can't work out where he is taking me. *If he wants to fire me, he would have done that after the first drink. It can't be a promotion—I have just been promoted ...*

"*Kampai*," he says once again, raising his glass as soon as he has finished pouring a third round.

At this point, I stop trying to understand where he is heading, as I am too drunk to do the math.

For the first time, I notice his soft, fatherly features and reassuring eyes.

"Sala-san, I believe something has been bothering you lately, and I would like to help."

His fatherly features and concern hit exactly the right button, and though a heart-to-heart with someone at his level is not the norm, I look into my half-empty glass, and it all comes pouring out—my failed marriage ... the Latino men in the airport executive lounges ... the crash landing ... the longing for a baby ... moving in with Mrs. Toda ...

The first thing I see when I wake up is a bright white light. It takes me another moment before I recognize Dharma lying against the tip of my nose, his dazzling white fur pressed against my face. His tail must have knocked my head and woken me up. My eyes are heavy, and I'm without a doubt experiencing a massive hangover.

Beyond the headlines, I remember very little of my confessions to Mr. Hashimoto and nothing of what came after. The fact that, whatever was said cannot be taken back is strangely comforting. I have no idea what the consequences will be, but for the first time since the crash landing episode, I feel less anxious.

Entertained by Dharma's playfulness, I sit up on the futon, take him in my arms, and hug him with a sudden burst of love. Dharma stretches his feet and surrenders his warm body to my arms.

"I am going to have a baby," I whisper to him.

Chapter 27: Getting Out There

I am *vastly* relieved that I am neither fired nor treated any differently after my full exposure at Mr. Hashimoto's office. It seems, on the contrary, to have met the Japanese ethics code; namely, the clear cut between such alcohol-induced confessions and work. This probably explains, in a way, what Mr. Hashimoto had in mind when he got me drunk in the first place.

Since my crash landing episode, I've avoided flights as much as possible. I even avoid *thinking* of them. Long-distance flights have been completely off the table for the successive two quarters since my return, which has been quite reasonable, considering the mileage Mr. Kobayashi and I covered during that three-week business trip. Still, I know that I can't avoid them for eternity, a thought that nags at me from time to time.

Then, a few days after my confession to both Mr. Hashimoto and to Dharma, I decide it's time to call and tell my mother. What I did not take into consideration was that she would now be calling me every single day, mesmerized by the idea she can finally be a grandmother. Unlike Dharma and Mr. Hashimoto who, as far as I can recall, has no real opinion on the matter, my mother not only has an opinion but is now on a mission. This is finally her chance to settle her status issues with her friends from the Hadassah Women's organization.

Her only child is thirty-seven, divorced, living in Japan, and providing her with no grandchildren to brag about. Now that I have sparked her imagination, she is determined to find me a successful Jewish divorcee ready for a second round.

"I hope you have lost some weight living in that godforsaken temple," she even added as the finale to our conversation last night.

Truth is, I didn't even consider how I am going to have a baby, whether I want to do it alone or with someone. Whether I want to build a family in the U.S. or continue the life I have kind of built for myself in Japan. Well, *kind of* does take into consideration that I have moved in with a singing widow of a Buddhist priest. Then come the thoughts of how I can possibly juggle life as a single mother in Japan in my position and how my firm will take it. Will they even accept it? These questions are overwhelming, and my nightly calls with my mom are sometimes simply more than I can handle.

The good thing is that I feel more alive now that I am actually facing these issues head-on. I feel as if options have opened well more accurately, like my mind has opened to so many options. That is, of course, how I see it on the days when I feel optimistic. When I don't really know how to take it all in, I simply decide to be deterministic about it, to shift my life motto from: *do what you need to do* to *what needs to happen happens*.

Chapter 28: A Leaping Golden Carp

A few days after my grand baby reveal, I actually mention to my mother that I am considering a sperm donation. I can't say that it was easy for me to word this out to her. I assume it is the first time in my life I ever said the word *sperm* to her. She is less surprised than I expected, almost as if she was waiting for me to say it.

Then, in a practical and poised voice, as if trying also to justify this odd mode of conversation to herself, she says, "Many career women do that these days. It is just part of the modern way of life."

By using the words "do that," she makes it all sound so technical, dampening my spirits instantly.

Then my father adds his usual motto, "Darling, do what you need to do."

And although I expected that from him, I'm still in awe at the range of issues his motto can be made to fit. Somehow, the excitement that their only daughter may soon be a mother is replaced by a dose of hard-core rationalization.

It's not that a sperm donation is my first choice. I would love for Prince Charming to knock on my door and to have this all figured out for me, but I have to admit that I'm left feeling somewhat orphaned by my parents' choice of wording.

Then, this morning, after an early breakfast, Mrs. Toda dresses me up in a blue wrap top and a conical straw hat. She has invited me to a rice planting festival in a village near Kamakura, the old Japanese capital with the Daibutsu, the huge sitting Buddha.

Every June, since her husband was a child, his family would gather in Kamakura, their hometown, for the rice planting. When he passed, Mrs. Toda vowed to continue this tradition for as long as she can actually stand on two feet. Just hearing this prologue from her, I cannot but be honored to be asked to tag along for the adventure.

We take the train to Kamakura, and I am surprised, as always, how no one looks my way. Me, in a blue wrap top with a conical straw hat in hand. *Wouldn't you think I look a bit out of context? I definitely feel as if I have entered the train in a costume.*

As we arrive at the station, we find ourselves walking among a similarly dressed crowd in the direction of the rice fields. Many people join the rice planting, including close and distant relatives of Mrs. Toda's husband, and the mutual greetings are endless.

Finally, we all gather by the rice paddies where we change into long, black, split-toe, frog-like boots. In my excitement, I take a few quick photos of my feet, sending them to Yuki with a text, saying, *Check out my new Gucci boots.*

The fields are divided into plots, covered with water and separated by narrow paths. From a bird's-eye view, it surely looks like an incredible maze. An altar has been erected in front of the fields, and a silver-haired Shinto priest waves a purifying wand over our heads as we bow in front of him, ready to set to work. Then, at the first chance I get, I come as close as I can to the altar. These altars are always so beautiful. I love every opportunity I have to see them up close.

The altar is constructed of light wooden shelves, which are filled with a variety of colorful fruits and vegetables, fresh fish, and other gifts of nature; everything set up so diligently. And, although they are in the middle of nowhere, it feels as if they belong. I have to admit that this specific display is spectacular. I find it hard to detach my eyes from it, as if it was meant to lure me in so that I can find some peace in its perfection.

The ritual begins, and we unanimously clap our hands together, calling on the spirits to join us. The priest recites some prayers, we clap again for the spirits to depart, and then head into the rice fields.

The earth is wet, and it feels like it gently embraces my two-toed feet. The mud is so soothing, as if I can take shelter in the nourishing soil under the pounding sun. I love it! The water is cold and refreshing, as well, so we gently immerse our bare hands and plant the sacred rice under the tips of our toes.

I can totally get frogs now. Who wants to sit in an air-conditioned office all day? This is totally it! I feel like I'm connecting to that child in me who didn't have many chances to stand in a pool of mud. I can actually see myself doing this every day ... Well, maybe not *every* day.

I get out of my head and look around, realizing the

silence and dedication of all the men and women, toddlers, and seniors. It's magical. I plant some rice and, from time to time, stretch my back then gaze at those around me, wearing conical straw hats, all fully engaged in the task at hand. There is something really peaceful about the fact that people actually take a day, dress up in the worst looking outfit, and take part in what feels like a humble retreat to the basics—planting your rice, meeting up with family members, showing appreciation for nature and tradition.

Besides my sudden desire to become a mom, I can't recall when I last thought about the value of family, nature, or tradition. Suddenly, I feel this undesired sadness and realize that, for the first time in many years, I actually desperately miss my parents.

As if she can read my thoughts and longing, Mrs. Toda lifts her eyes and smiles at me like a mother looking out for her child. I smile back at her, and though I am wrapped with a sudden feeling of loneliness, I'm somewhat comforted.

We work our way through the silky mud and, just as I kneel down to plant another stem of rice, I see it and my euphoria is shattered. Brown, long, and quicker than my thoughts.

In an instant, all the positive energy around me dissolves into its unwelcome, slick, sinful existence ...

"A SNAKE!" I yell out in panic, breaking the utopic silence.

I don't remember when I last ran that fast. In a split-second, I am out on the footpath, making my way through the labyrinth like a mouse on steroids in a lab. I run and run, hopping on my two-toed feet, trying to touch the ground as little as possible, from one rice paddy to the next, not daring to look back. I run as fast as I can, feeling the unbearable tension every time I grudgingly land. I run and run and run.

"At last, a familiar face!" I yell out, and before I can fully comprehend who he is or how I know him, I shut my eyes and lift my body into the air, like one of those Chinese kung-fu characters, and park straight in his arms.

There is a moment of silence, as if the soundtrack of the horror movie has been cut off right at the climax. I feel I am safe in these arms but would rather die than open my eyes or say a word.

"You again, landing in my arms," the man whispers, amused.

I shut my eyes even tighter to try to comprehend who on earth this could be. Then I slowly open one eye after the other.

I am relieved that the familiar face is at least not one of my clients, yet I am still unable to figure out who he is, nor mutter a word, and I can feel myself blushing more than I thought I ever could.

"Hello, Sala-san. I am happy to see you, too!" he continues then starts laughing. The laughter instantly reveals who he is. I recognize it, as it is just as he laughed the first time I saw him at Mrs. Toda's temple grounds with Dharma in his arms.

"By the way, my name is Nobu," he adds, carefully setting me back on my feet.

I take a moment, staring at him, not knowing really what to say. "There was a snake," I finally reply in my most innocent tone, trying to justify my existence after failing to dissolve into thin air.

Nobu simply moves on as if it is his daily practice, explaining that snakes are not uncommon in rice fields and that they are believed to bring good luck.

Go figure! I think to myself, another thing no one considered to mention. Actually, it is probably for the best that I didn't know in advance.

"Are the girls here?" I ask, trying to divert my attention from the disturbing image of the long, limbless reptile still crawling through my thoughts.

"The girls are over there with Junko, preparing lunch boxes for the workers in the fields," he says, pointing at a group of women and young children about a hundred feet away.

"Junko-chan!" He raises his hand and calls out toward her.

She and the girls wave back at us enthusiastically.

"Junko looks after the girls so that I can catch ladies who jump into my arms," says Nobu, smiling, his eyes playfully scanning mine. "Come; let's grab some lunch."

I follow him toward the pile of lunch boxes. He picks out two and, before I can say a word, Junko and the girls are upon us. I greet them with smiles, and Hiromi, the older of the two, hands me a box and asks me to join the fun by filling some lunch boxes with them.

An audience of elderly women with question-mark shaped postures, due to immensely crooked backs, uniformed straw hats, and uneven teeth watch me suspiciously from their low-crouching positions.

After filling up a few lunch boxes, Nobu turns to them and, in his deep voice, asks that we be excused. Relieved to get out of the spotlight, I hand Hiromi a half-filled lunch box, give a friendly bow to the curious crowd, and then follow Nobu. He suggests we take a walk out of the rice fields, and I simply can't refuse being offered an escape route.

He leads us back to where we first gathered and to my plain, old, five-toe accompanying shoes. I never assumed I would appreciate the additional toe space as much as I do.

We head back in the direction of the station then turn toward a pebble path. The pebble path curves right for a while and, eventually, the rice fields are out of sight. We walk along in silence, the pebbles beneath our feet generating a relaxing soundtrack underneath us. The refreshing scent of the pine trees above us cleanses my thoughts, and as I remove my straw hat and let my hair down, the fresh air blowing over my face feels so good. Next, we come across a modest Shinto shrine. My senses are alert to the subtle but calming change of scenery and ambience.

When stroll toward the entrance to the shrine, a small pond with the biggest, most colorful carps is revealed before our eyes. Taking Nobu's lead, I sit down on a large rock overlooking the pond, and we gaze at the water, a light breeze accompanying our private performance. It is the first time I have ever seen carps jump, and it is more amusing than I expected it to be. Just for a few moments, I feel like a child at the zoo, taking it all in as if they were there to entertain me. But, just as I fully relax, a large, golden carp leaps into the air then dives back into the pond, splashing me in the face. Nobu looks at me, and there goes his familiar laugh again.

After collecting my ego, I join him in laughter. I haven't laughed this much for a very long time, and I am fully present in the moment. Nobu laughs, and I feel more and more relaxed. His deep but somewhat wild laughter is refreshing after spending so many years among so many well-contained Japanese.

"Don't tell me a splashing carp brings good luck, as well?" I say, pushing back my wet hair like a model in a shampoo commercial. "Next thing you know, a bird will poop all over me, and I will truly be the luckiest woman on earth!" I add with a giggle.

This time, I find myself entertained on my own, realizing that Nobu hasn't registered my last comment. *I guess you don't do the poop thing in Japan*, I conclude, witnessing slight confusion in Nobu's deep, dark eyes. And, although he seems to not have followed my last comment, he finally—after a short, uneventful pause—smiles at me. Then he takes out a small handkerchief from his pocket and, without warning, gently wipes away a few of the drops making their way down the side of my neck. I freeze in place, trying to act as if his gentle touch hasn't awakened all my senses at once.

"Here is your lunch box," he says, unfreezing me as I melt back into reality.

He hands me one of the two lunch boxes he previously took from the pile. We unwrap the white paper covering the wooden boxes and take the chopsticks out of their small white envelopes, pulling them apart.

"*Itadakimasu*," we say together, tucking into our seemingly simple meal with great appetite.

The wind is softly ruffling my hair and, with every bite, I feel more grounded and more at peace.

When we finish eating, Nobu collects our lunch boxes,

wraps them together, and then stands before me. He offers me his hand and pulls me to my feet.

I find myself standing very close to him for an instant, my body stiffens, and the warmth of his body occupying the space between us vibrates with energy. Then Nobu releases my hand and spins on the spot, pointing toward the gate of the shrine.

"Shall we?" he asks, and I smile.

I follow him, taken once again by his strong, powerful arms, which fill the sleeves of his uniform. We stop at the stone basin in front of the shrine and, as if reading my thoughts, he rolls up his sleeves.

The clear, purifying water runs through his fingers and a few playful drops make their way up his elbow. As soon as he finishes the ritual hand-washing, he passes me the long bamboo hand-washing utensil, and I, too, run the water through my fingers, feeling his intense eyes on me.

We meander toward the gate, stop at its entrance, bow in front of the shrine, and then step into the compound.

"Come. This is what I wanted to show you," says Nobu, grabbing my hand again and pulling me toward the back of the shrine.

I am a little puzzled by this unexpected maneuver, but then he points at a small traditional house that looks just like one of the houses I once saw on a samurai movie set.

"This is where Mrs. Toda's husband and my father were raised," he says, pointing proudly at the small house. "My father is the last Shinto priest in the family. His brother, Mrs. Toda's husband, as you know, became a Buddhist priest."

Only now do I understand that Nobu is Mrs. Toda's

nephew.

He then continues, "I love our Japanese traditions, but becoming a priest is not for me. I prefer to design temples and shrines rather than pray and hold ceremonies in them. Maybe one day one of my girls will become an architect, as well, and then I will have started a traditional lineage of my own." He smiles to himself, and I can see he is thinking of them. They are so sweet; why would he not be smiling?

I look at him, thinking how unusual it is to meet someone both practical and spiritual.

"And how did your family react to your uncle becoming a Buddhist priest?" I ask curiously after a short pause.

"As you see, in Japan, we do our best to enjoy all our traditions," he concludes the conversation with a typical Japanese answer, again offering a view into the positive side of things, elegantly maneuvering through the subject.

By now, at the gate of the shrine, are dozens of people. They have just finished working in the fields and are sitting and enjoying their lunches. Kids are laughing and running up and down the pebble path, which connects the newly planted rice fields with the shady, cool, peaceful grounds of the shrine where Nobu's father, Mrs. Toda's brother-in law, serves as a Shinto priest.

A light breeze pats my warm cheeks, and I close my eyes, enhancing the sensation even further.

On hearing the young kids giggles of joy grow louder, I open my eyes again. Nobu is standing beside me, smiling at me, and directing me elegantly back to the shrine gate.

Chapter 29: Sweeping The Pebbles

"*Biru*," Mrs. Toda mumbles, slightly raising her eyebrows like an eager teenager with a fake ID.

"B-e-e-r?" I repeat, trying to confirm her answer to my question of how she would like to celebrate her birthday.

"*Hai, biru!*" Mrs. Toda nods in approval, eyes opening wide as she breaks into a charming, childlike smile I have never seen on her before.

"Is there any special type of beer you would like?" I ask, intrigued by her choice.

Perhaps she wants to taste some rare foreign brand.

Mrs. Toda stares at me blankly. After more than five years of living in Japan, I have become very familiar with the blank-eyed stare, meaning she has no idea what kind of beer she would like.

It turns out that, on her seventy-second birthday, she is hoping to fulfill a very long-lived, teenage fantasy—having beer for the very first time.

So, here I am after a day at the office, birthday hat on head, sitting and waiting for Mrs. Toda to return from her karaoke club meeting.

Work has become more relaxed for me lately, though my hours and evenings out with my team or with clients hasn't slowed much. Somehow, the fact that I haven't traveled for a while and the feeling that I'm about to embark on a greater journey—having a child—keeps me focused. It's as if I have never felt the feeling of determination as I do now. Determination for something greater than being the star of my own *Devil Wears Prada* movie.

Mrs. Toda arrives just after her regular hour with a sweet, content smile on her face. I greet her on the deck with an array of Japan's finest beers and a variety of America's finest snacks—Pringles!

As she walks up the path, her eyes widen, and I can see her excitement. I take a few steps, hands behind my back, and when I am just in front of her, I hand her a matching birthday hat and offer her a seat next to me on the deck. She sits herself down on her knees, settles the hat atop her bouncy gray bangs, and places her tiny hands on her thighs, ready to start.

"Happy birthday!" I exclaim cheerfully, this time revealing a tiny box from behind my back and handing it to her.

She accepts the gift with two hands, lays the small box in front of her, and unwraps it carefully.

"It is a beer bottle opener," I explain as I notice her examining it with some uncertainty. "Just in case, after seventy-two years, you suddenly find the taste of beer irresistible," I add playfully. I then show her that I had it inscribed with the words, "*Some Things Taste Better with Time*," hoping she finds these words either comforting or amusing, depending on how she relates to the bitter liquid and to the fact that she finally gets to live her dream.

Mrs. Toda lifts her gaze toward me and bows her head lightly and somewhat bashfully.

I wonder for an instant if she can even relate in any way to what I wrote.

"Pringles?" I ask, playing hostess as I hold out the plate toward her. She delicately picks out one potato chip and lifts it toward her mouth.

"*Itadakimasu*," she says then takes a tiny bite of the single potato chip in her hand.

I smile, amused by how only Japanese women can avoid shoving a whole potato chip into their mouths at once, and then I bow my head in return.

I pour her first ever glass of beer!

There is a moment of silence between us, and then she finally extends both hands and lifts the glass up.

"*Kampai!*" she says.

I reply, "Cheers!"

I watch her in anticipation as she tilts the glass toward her mouth, the liquid passing through the foam and slipping slowly between her lips. She takes two additional sips then lays the glass down on the deck in front of her.

I examine her, concerned that maybe her decades-long fantasy has been shattered by the bitter and unrewarding first taste of beer. But then she lifts her eyes, and I spy the same childlike smile I first saw this morning.

Three bottles later, and she is singing! A sip or two more, and we are both dancing some traditional Japanese dance that she insists on teaching me while she sings its repetitive tune. By the fourth bottle, we are trying in vain to get ahold of

Dharma, who passes by, examining us suspiciously. Dharma refuses to take any part of our celebration.

We know so little about each other, I think to myself as we sit ourselves down to rest, our legs swinging from the edge of the deck.

All I know about Mrs. Toda is from Akiko, the woman at the pharmacy, and from Nobu. I know that, at the age of five, she lost her parents in the Osaka bombings of 1945 and was raised in a Buddhist temple in Osaka. I know that she is the widow of a Buddhist priest, that her husband was raised in Kamakura and was Nobu's father's brother, that she sings karaoke, and that she takes care of the temple and its surroundings as if her late husband was about to return at any given moment.

As if she can read my mind, Mrs. Toda suddenly says, "My father worked in a ceramic workshop. He made tea bowls for tea masters. In the evenings, he liked to drink beer." Her long pause is justified by the fact that this is the very first time she has shared with me any personal information regarding her life.

After a few moments of silence, she then continues, telling me that the smell of beer always reminds her of her father and that her mother always sang to her, which is why she, too, enjoys singing. She apparently grew up in a tiny home and shares that her mother fed her black seaweed to keep her hair black and shiny. She goes into detail, telling me how she and her mother used to visit the public baths down the street, and her mother loved washing and brushing her hair.

I can see how her story fills her with warmth mixed with

a hint of sadness, but then she talks and giggles in her dignified yet unassuming way, and I feel so close to her and grateful that she took me in.

She goes on to tell me that, just a few days before she turned seventeen, her late husband, then aged thirty and on a Buddhist pilgrimage, visited the temple where she was living. They met one morning while she was sweeping the pebbles off the path, and he told her of his calling to spread the teachings of the Buddha. She recalls being impressed by his spirituality and his determination. He promised her that, at the end of his pilgrimage, he would come back and marry her and take her back with him to his hometown near Tokyo. She waited for him, sweeping the pebbles off the path every morning.

Then, on the day she turned eighteen, he returned, looking quite different from the man she remembered—his body slimmer, his head closely shaven, and his eyes more mature. When they got married, he gave her a home and inspired her with his kindness. She, in return, vowed to be his loyal and devoted wife to the day she died.

Around midnight, we find ourselves in the kitchen, exhausted. We collapse into our regular seats, namely the pillows that are spread around the dining table on the tatami floor.

Mrs. Toda serves us both cubes of chilled tofu, seasoned with soy sauce and a little grated ginger, one of my favorite Japanese dishes, which I call "a Japanese hot fudge sundae."

As we silently revert to our hot fudge sundaes, I look up at Mrs. Toda. I can see that she is truly happy.

Chapter 30: A Gift

Talk to them. Tell them how important they are to you. Tell them you could never have gotten where you are without them ... Be kind and compassionate ...
...
...
...
It's not working...
Try smiling at them.
No, not like that! An inner smile, a smile no one sees other than you ... Positive thoughts can move things, right?
Not working. Okay, move!

I simply can't figure out how two functioning feet of a thirty-something-year-old can suddenly go completely numb.

Don't start sweating. The guests will notice!

I've been having an intense, inner discussion now for what seems like an eternity, but I can't seem to gain control.

Why the hell aren't they moving?

My feet are dead after sitting on my knees for the past forty minutes. I cannot move them an inch. I don't think the guests have realized it yet. As long as they are enjoying this endless tea ceremony, last thing I want is to spoil the fun.

I am way past my cue to get up, but I don't see how that is ever going to happen. I wonder how many people have been left to die like this, stuck on their knees after hosting a tea ceremony. I can't be the first to get stuck in place. That alone would be a reason to die.

I can see from the question mark in Mrs. Toda's eyes that she is on to me. *Yep, I knew it!* She is shuffling toward me, trailing her feet in their white, two-toed socks, and now she is kneeling beside me ... I hope she is not planning to clear the dishes instead of me. That would be embarrassing. Okay, this is a bit odd, maybe even odder than being stuck this way forever—she is reaching for my feet.

Mrs. Toda grabs my ankles and bends my toes back until they practically crack. I feel like a chicken whose wishbone has been torn apart while still alive and kicking.

"Argh!" I let out a cry of shock, mixed with a respectable level of distress. *She could have given me some type of warning. Jeez.*

But it works! I finally begin to feel my feet again. And in accordance with the Japanese code of ethics, while I yelled out in pain, none of the guests even blinked nor turned in my direction. Yet again, I've been spared from losing face in public. Or perhaps they are simply deep in meditation ... or maybe they are actually a bunch of sadists.

I take a deep breath, assume a subtle smile, and try to contemplate my next move.

Now, I somehow need to get up from this awkward position elegantly, a tea bowl carefully resting in both hands. Okay, if I concentrate hard enough on the task ...

After running the moves through my head a dozen or more times, I finally work the magic and lift myself carefully as I've been trained. First, I bend my toes back, then I put one foot forward and allow the center of my body to lift me up like a puppet on a string. Most importantly, I remember to keep my tongue in while doing the moves, since I have a tendency to stick it out when I am concentrating—*not elegant!*

I drag them slowly as they seem now to weigh twice the weight of the rest of my body. This actually works well with my task in hand as I am constrained by the ritual and by the tight binding of my *yukata*. Finally, I slip out of the tea ceremony room and into the service area just in time to let out a desperate cry. I roll my eyes and kneel to try to massage my ankles, which are half numb and half in pain.

I am serving tea. Me, of all people. How did that happen? Well, to cut a long story short, after moving in with Mrs. Toda, I offered to pay rent, but she refused. I then asked her if there was anything I could do to repay her for all her kindness and for accommodating me. At first, she wouldn't even consider it. I insisted and, at any given opportunity, offered once more to contribute my share. A short while after we celebrated her birthday, she suggested teaching me the tea ceremony so that, when summer came around, I could help her entertain guests on the weekends.

As an executive, I am the one who is usually served tea and, as a divorcee, I am spared the pleasure of serving tea to a husband who has caught a cold but is convinced he is in the throes of death. The concept of serving tea is the furthest thing from my reality, but it seemed the very least I could do after all Mrs. Toda has done for me. So, I am served tea during the days and serve tea myself to others during the evenings.

Contrary to the role of serving tea in the Japanese business world, which is clearly a woman's role, most masters of tea ceremony are actually men. After all, it is considered a prestigious, full-time occupation, an art and way of life for those who master it.

I know the tea ceremony is not about serving tea ... Well, not all about it. If it were, then the Japanese would be masters of complicating things. Well, in some respect they actually are—look at their language. But I realize the tea ceremony does have something magical about it, despite the pain I feel right now.

So, for the past six weeks, every evening, no matter how late I get home from work, except, of course, for Wednesdays, which is karaoke night, Mrs. Toda gives me a lesson in the art of the tea ceremony.

Aside from its strict and repeated, almost dance-like sequence of moves, I have learned that the tea ceremony consists of many other forms of Japanese art. Mrs. Toda has shown me her handmade bowls with colors and textures reflecting the different seasons or the atmosphere she chooses from as a host for a specific serving.

She sets calligraphies and flower arrangements in a niche in the tea ceremony room, mindful to mirror the desired mood, like lyrics complementing the music. Following her diligently setting the mood is thrilling, as if entering a parallel universe where words cannot reflect such subtleties.

From Mrs. Toda, I learned that it takes decades of practice and a deep connection to nature and your inner self to make a true tea master. And so, not only am I serving tea, I am also sharing an old tradition as a young and sometimes, like today for example, helpless student with a long path ahead. Hopefully, being a foreigner cuts me some slack with the guests.

My heart misses a beat when I enter the back room and find Nobu standing quietly in the opposite doorway, holding a large paper package in his hands.

"What are you doing here?" I ask, caught a bit off balance, trying to maintain a casual appearance and suddenly realizing how rude that must have sounded. I reveal a friendly smile to try to be more welcoming, yet still battle to regain some feeling in my feet. Sort of like a squid trying to balance on two limbs on an ice-skating rink.

Nobu stands there, watching me closely with his solid silence, while I finally balance myself enough to give him my full attention.

"This is for you." He steps forward and hands me the paper packed package with both hands.

I hold the package, staring at it quietly, not sure what to say.

"It is a gift from Junko. She made you a *yukata* for the summer. She was not sure whether you have one, and she hopes you like it."

I stand there with the package, speechless. Well, at least until I finally gather the courage to raise my eyes from it. "Wow. I don't know what to say …" which seems like the only thing I can muster right now.

"There are fireworks in Kamakura next week. If you are free, please come and watch them with us. Junko can dress you in the *yukata*, and we can enjoy the fireworks together."

He scans my eyes carefully and adds a light smile.

"I love fireworks," I say before actually considering his invitation.

An odd, undeserving feeling starts creeping through me at receiving a gift from Junko, who I have never really spoken to, realizing that all my interactions with Nobu seem to include some level of flirting.

"So, you must come. Junko and the girls will be so happy to see you," Nobu concludes decisively.

We stand there, gazing at each other for a few moments, until I suddenly remember that Mrs. Toda and the guests are still waiting.

"I have to go back and help Mrs. Toda with the guests," I say then turn around, placing the package as gently as I can in the corner of the room. I then reach up to a shelf full of ceramic dishes and carefully choose a fresh bowl.

"That is one of my favorites," Nobu says, delighted with my choice. "I made that bowl last year on one of the hottest days of summer."

Heat rises to my cheeks, and my hands grow moist. "I didn't know it was yours," I say, lowering my gaze from his gratified expression. I raise my eyes for an instant and add, "Please thank Junko for her kind gift." Then I bow my head slightly before returning to the tea ceremony room.

As I slip away, I can feel Nobu's eyes still watching me from behind.

When the guests have finally left, I return to the service area, part of me hoping that Nobu will still be there yet knowing it is not likely. The room is empty, but I can feel his presence, maybe even smell his lingering scent.

I pick out a few bowls from the shelf and turn them over, checking for his signature seal. I discover that he actually made quite a few of them, even some of my favorites. I run my fingers over his bowls, feeling their uneven textures, excited to have learned something new and unexpected about him. I picture his masculine arms, wide neck, and strongly built shoulders, and just for a moment, I thirst to be as surrounded and raw in his hands as the bowls once were.

It is a warm summer evening, and I am exhausted from my long day yet excited I've received a gift, like a child who has been allowed to stay up late on a school night.

I place the bowls back on the shelf and shuffle to the corner of the room. Kneeling down carefully, I pick up the paper package with Junko's gift in both hands. I take another moment to examine it, eager to tear it open.

Just then, Mrs. Toda steps into the storage room to say goodnight. I bow to her and thank her for the evening.

As soon as she leaves, I drag my weary feet back to Sala's Room, place the gift on my white, fluffy carpet, and then slide the door shut. Finally, I can feel the long day taking its toll. I open the *yukata* I was wearing for the tea ceremony and let it slip off my body and onto the tatami, feeling an instant relief. I change into a comfortable, baggy T-shirt, sit down on the carpet in front of the package, and pull it toward me, opening it carefully.

The more I inspect the *yukata*, the more beautiful it appears. It is bright red, with large, lush flowers. I lay it out gently next to me, mesmerized by its vigor and colors. Its *Obi*, the sash of the *yukata*, is no less impressive.

A wave of anxiety hits me, and I become aware of my

mixed feelings. On the one hand, Japan is opening up to me through Mrs. Toda and Nobu like never before, and I am grateful to be seeing and experiencing so many genuine parts of its culture and tradition. On the other hand, I have a very strong feeling that I am falling for Nobu.

Chapter 31: Fire Flowers

"Oh God, noooo!"

"I'm okay! I'm fine. Don't mind me! Go on. I will catch up soon!" I shout out as convincingly as I can while struggling to pick up both the bicycle and myself for the third time since I got on it.

They say you never forget how to ride a bicycle. I am living proof that this is a myth. An evil myth. I don't know what I was thinking. If I just wanted to impress them, I could have chosen one of my other skills, like making dolphin sounds or singing the alphabet backward.

Riding a bike is so routine in Japan that I could have just given it a miss and no one would have batted an eyelid, not suspecting for a moment. Instead, I dove headfirst into a massive rice field.

The second we turned the corner and I saw the slope, I knew I couldn't stop. Next thing I knew, the fields at the end of the road were getting closer and closer, and there was no way I was going to get this bicycle to stop in time.

Being rescued by five- and seven-year-old girls is sort of humiliating, especially when their high-pitched giggles spread for miles around, grabbing the attention of the evenly pacing Japanese heading from the train station back home.

"Have you ever heard the sound of a dolphin?" I plead, trying to drift their attention from my weak trait to my truly unique one, as the girls desperately try and fail to pull me up.

I begin making my pitiful dolphin squeaks, and only when they stop their laughter and take a step back, do I realize that I've lost any last remnant of dignity and they are actually frightened as hell.

A large shadow looms over me, and a huge hand grabs my arm, finally pulling me to my feet.

"You rescue me once again," I say, looking up at Nobu with my best feminine wiles.

"It will be easier to watch the sun set if we walk," he replies, his eyes smiling. I've come to love his smile.

Once again, how very Japanese to find the good in any situation, making an excuse to help me save face yet sounding so convincing.

Safely out of the rice field, I follow him and his younger daughter, while the older, Hiromi, walks aside me protectively, perhaps hoping to save me from falling back into the warm, silky field. It feels strange to have such a small, delicate hand holding mine, and for a moment, I wish Hiromi was my own.

I surrender to the thought that I am actually committed to having a child. It suddenly feels so real, so natural. I've never been so eager.

Last week, the day after Nobu's surprise visit during the tea ceremony, I finally gave my parents a date. I decided it would be right to try to return home for Thanksgiving, like in the old days.

Now that I can actually almost smell the joy of a child's hand in mine, I also know I will find the strength to overcome my fear of flying, at least for that one flight, which could make my life ever so meaningful.

We stop pacing, and my mind shifts back to the present. With the sunset comes that special moment when heaven and earth become one, and we all stand still, silently gazing out beyond the nicely growing rice in the fields.

As we continue around the bend, I recognize the short, familiar pebble path that Nobu and I took on the day of the rice planting. Passing the shrine, we soon arrive at Nobu's father's modest home.

Junko is waiting for us at the entrance, and she greets us with warmth, as if we arrived after a long, tiring pilgrimage, offering us chilled *oolong* tea and peeled grapes. *Yes, the Japanese peel grapes—tomatoes, too!*

We drink slowly and enjoy the grapes and cool shelter of their home. The girls don't spare me and go on giggling about my recent fall. I break and admit to my weakness and head-on dive into the rice fields, and we all laugh.

Once we have concluded our refreshments, Junko asks me to follow her to another room so she can dress me in the *yukata* that she made me, which I brought with me. The girls follow us excitedly.

As Junko dresses me, the two girls do their best to mimic her moves and dress each other in their own festive *yukata*. From time to time, Junko turns to them and guides them in a soft, loving voice.

Junko attends to me with such care, observing every

detail of the ritual, dressing and making me feel like a bride on her special day. It is the first time I've really seen her up close, and I notice how smooth her skin is and how bright her eyes are. They have that same hidden smile as in Nobu's eyes. I can appreciate what Nobu finds in her kind hands, serene presence, and tender voice.

But maybe she is too peaceful for him? a voice nags me from within, and I quickly push that thought away.

The wide, impressive *obi* is the last detail before Junko steps back and surveys my overall appearance. After a careful review, her eyes meet mine, and she starts clapping her hands in joy. The girls, who by now are sitting and playing with each other's hair, get up and join the applause in excitement.

I turn toward the mirror. The *yukata* is even more vibrant than I remembered it, and it fits me perfectly. I turn back to Junko, feeling a strong desire to hug her, but before I can say a word, the girls jump between us, dragging Nobu in by the hands.

Dressed in a simple, white *yukata*, covered with black, fan-like shapes, Nobu, extremely handsome, smiles at me with a proud, content look in his eyes. I smile back happily.

Izumi, the younger of the girls, picks up a small, colorful paper fan from the tatami mat and hands it to me, while Hiromi grabs my hand and drags me toward the door. Before I can even thank Junko properly, she hands me a pair of *geta*, the sadistic Japanese wooden flip-flops. Then, as soon as I have slipped them on, she pulls me by the hand, out of the house, and toward the shrine.

"Thank you, Junko-san!" I shout, hoping she can hear me from within the house.

Trying to keep my balance on these wooden objects of torture that the Japanese insist are shoes, we move past the shrine and in the direction of the carp pond.

Hiromi suddenly lets go of my hand and runs ahead toward an older man who is climbing up the pebble path in our direction. It's Nobu's father, the Shinto priest, and he is also dressed in a plain black and white *yukata*. I would never have recognized him had Hiromi not run toward him. He seems older than I remember him in front of the altar on the rice planting day.

I want to tell him that I saw the rice fields earlier, and that they seem to be growing well, but for fear of raising the topic of my small bicycle incident, I just bow toward him, mumbling some basic Japanese pleasantries. He stops just in front of me and bows likewise. Soon, Nobu and Izumi show up and stand alongside Hiromi and me.

"Junko will not be joining us for the fireworks," Nobu says then apologizes on Junko's behalf before I have the chance to ask.

It seems odd to me that she has chosen not to join us, and I'm hopeful I didn't cause her any discomfort. I quickly let go of the thought. Her presence is nonetheless felt due to this beautiful *yukata* she made me, although I cannot help wondering why she would go out of her way to give me such a magnificent and thoughtful gift.

Hiromi and Izumi each grab one of my hands, and we all follow the pebble path back down to the fields.

A festive crowd dressed in dazzling *yukatas* gathers for the fireworks. Booths selling chilled drinks, squid puffs resembling donuts, and grilled skewers of sweet-sauce-covered rice balls are set up at the entrance of the viewing area, giving off that familiar, nostalgic smell of a Japanese summer night. The fireworks explode above us in a paradise of colors and shapes, filling the limitless skies and justifying their Japanese name, *hanabi*, literally, *fire flowers*.

This is one of the happiest days of my life.

Chapter 32: A Slap In The Face

On September 11, the same exact date the lives of millions of individuals changed forever, the day on which Naomi disappeared beyond the flames of the World Trade Center, Mrs. Toda passed away.

It was a Saturday, and I had kicked off the day in my usual spot at the small knee-high table but alone. Not only was Mrs. Toda not there with my breakfast, as she was every day, even the smell of miso soup was lacking.

After a few long moments, I got up and walked toward the front deck, peeking in at the reception hall, the family altar, and the bathroom, but they were all empty. Finally, I strolled down the corridor to Mrs. Toda's bedroom.

Her door was closed.

I called out her name, but there was no answer. I went back to the dining room, hoping to find her there, eagerly expecting me, as usual.

Neither Mrs. Toda nor Dharma were anywhere in sight.

I looked around the kitchen, hoping to find a hint of her early morning presence, but the kitchen was spotless. I noticed for the first time that she had hung the beer bottle opener I gave her for her birthday on the wall by the sink.

Realizing I had no choice, I went back to her room and quietly opened the sliding door. Mrs. Toda was lying on her futon. Her eyes were closed. Dharma sat faithfully by her side.

"Toda-san?" I called out, but she lay there perfectly still. "Toda-san?" I called out again, just a bit louder, part of me still expecting her to answer.

She was as still as the air around her.

Hoping to wake her, I slowly sat down next to Dharma, but as soon as I touched her hand, I knew she was no longer with us.

Dharma and I both stared at Mrs. Toda in silence.

I am not sure how much time passed before I stood and went back to the dining room, sat down at the knee-high table, took a few deep breaths, and then called Yuki, asking him to come right over.

It was only when Yuki arrived and I looked into his caring eyes that the first tear rolled down my cheek, and once the tears started, they just wouldn't stop. Yuki notified the office that we would both take leave then contacted Nobu. The two of them took charge.

I spend most of the morning lying on the futon placed on my white carpet in my large, empty room.

September 11, the exact date that Naomi died, Mrs. Toda passes away. This goes over and over in my mind. I can simply not believe that two women of such significance to me died on the very same date.

Guests begin to arrive in the afternoon; mostly relatives of Nobu, as her husband's family was the only family she ever really knew. Some, I even recognize from the rice planting.

A Japanese-style wake is set up in the reception area. It is the first time I've ever attended any sort of wake. Jews don't sit in the presence of the dead, so I find the whole situation a bit spooky and weird. I feel like a zombie trapped and wrapped in layers of white sadness.

Platters of sushi and bottles of beer and saké are placed on an altar next to Mrs. Toda's coffin, and some are being consumed by the guests. I wonder whether Mrs. Toda is amused at being offered beer at her wake when she only recently tried it for the first time. I'm so glad that she had the chance to taste it with me while she was still alive and that she didn't have to lie here, craving the unattainable substance. I smile for a split-second, reconstructing in my thoughts some of the magical moments of her seventy-second birthday, grateful I had the opportunity to celebrate it with her.

Services are conducted at both ends of the reception hall. At one end, Nobu's father heads a Shinto-style ceremony, while on the other, Akira chants Buddhist sutras. They are showing full mutual tolerance for each other's faith, each determined in their own way to guard Mrs. Toda's body and soul from evil spirits.

I, however, feel unable to connect with anything around me. All the people in the temple and Mrs. Toda's unprecedented absence, I feel invaded. A pain in my chest spreads through my body like ink on rice paper. It is all so overwhelming, and I just want this nightmare to end. I want to start the day again, to wake up to another peaceful morning with Mrs. Toda's miso soup and Japanese pickled plums.

Dharma, too, is restless, circling around and around Mrs. Toda's coffin. At a certain point, I pick him up and take him out onto the deck. But he remains just as edgy.

Unwillingly, I let him go.

I feel weak and hungry. I realize that I haven't eaten all day. Then a wave of heat and humidity washes over my face.

I head back to the reception hall, recognizing that, given my current state, I am best off reconvening with the drunken mourners, the deceased guest of honor, and some remnants of raw fish lying on large, round platters. *Sashimi* isn't exactly what I would have chosen to eat right now, but the thought of going into the empty kitchen is even more depressing.

In the corridor on my way back to the reception hall, I find Nobu. I have been avoiding him for most of the day, as I feel I can't gather enough energy to confront anyone else's pain but mine. From his intense gaze, it seems that he has been looking for me. His face is red, and the smile in his eyes is gone. It is clear that he has had a fair amount to drink.

I know I cannot avoid him any longer, so I approach him, but before I can even look him back in the eyes, he grabs me by the waist and pushes me over to the dark-paneled wall.

I can't breathe.

His lips are shiny, and his hair is pushed back from the heat. He roughly takes my head in his hands and runs his manly fingers through my hair. Pressing his lips tightly to mine, his tongue cuts through my silence. I close my eyes, feeling defeated and overwhelmed by sadness while at the same time craving to be conquered, a deep sense of comfort in his alcohol-infused breath. But before I can fully surrender to my own longing for his uncontrollable lust, the pain in my chest takes over.

"Stop!" I snap, pushing him away then slapping him

across his already flushed cheeks with my sweaty hand.

He steps back, his eyes falling to the floor, and I run away down the long corridor to my room.

I spend the rest of the afternoon on my own. I am no longer just sad; I am also angry and disappointed. Mrs. Toda just passed away, and Junko is in the next room! *What was he thinking?*

A chill runs through me with the sensation of his strong hands running through my hair, his broad chest pushing against me. I lie down on my white furry carpet and stare at the ceiling, eyes watering again. My appetite is gone.

At a certain point, Yuki comes into my room and insists that I join him to take leave of the guests and of Mrs. Toda before she is taken away to be cremated.

The guests are already in the doorway. I look at them, perspiring in their black attire, most men tipsy, but all are ready to move on to the lively world beyond the temple gates. Akira stands out among the crowds with his shaved head and his gray, Buddhist robe.

I bow again and again, feeling odd to have earned a position that was not mine to earn. After all, I only lived with Mrs. Toda for less than a year, and now I am the chief mourner, parting from people she has known forever.

Nobu and Junko are the last to leave. I glance quickly at Nobu's face, just enough to make sure that I haven't left my mark. He doesn't even look my way. They bow politely, turn on their heels, and then leave.

I cry all night. From time to time, I wipe my eyes and call out to Dharma, hoping in vain that he might come and cheer me up. When I can no longer stand my own sobbing, I ring my parents.

During Ben and my first two years in Japan, my parents visited us three times. But once I started traveling more frequently to the U.S. and my father retired, they seemed to prefer holidays requiring less travel time and offering a more familiar cuisine. At first, I was disappointed by how easily they gave up on the idea of visiting their only daughter, even if she did live across the Pacific, but I soon learned not to expect too much and to make the most of their distinctive mom-and-pop love as it is, and whenever I can.

My mom answers the phone. She is sympathetic, repeating everything I say to my dad, who seems to be right next to her, and although the call is on speaker mode. I feel that, while they do want to be here for me, they are simply too far away to bridge the void.

The phone conversation starts with some reality therapy and quickly takes on a different tone. "Maybe you should consider coming home earlier than November," my mom starts then begins filling me in on the latest gossip from her Hadassah Women's reunion.

I hang up feeling even lonelier than before.

As the first signs of dawn seep through the gap at the bottom of my bedroom door, I lay my head on my pillow and finally close my eyes.

Chapter 33: The Will

Monday morning, at 6:30 a.m., my alarm clock goes off. By 8:30 a.m., I am dressed to kill and back at the office.

On my desk are sixteen memos addressed to all division heads, twelve contracts to review, five contracts to sign, three summaries of conference calls I need to read through, and two hundred and eighty-six emails in my inbox, new ones popping up by the minute.

My day begins with a budgetary meeting and two international conference calls. At noon, I am standing in the ramen shop down the street, slurping down noodles with a handful of grey-suited salary men, the only common denominator being our lack of time for a normal lunch break.

At 10:00 p.m., I am still at my desk.

Yuki approaches me carefully and asks if we can talk.

I sit up and turn his way, demolishing the chocolates and rice crackers that I bought from the vending machine in the lobby to keep me going through the long night ahead.

"Mrs. Toda left a will," I hear him say amidst the loud, crunching sounds echoing in my ears.

"Okay ..." I answer, mildly curious, largely in denial, but

still preoccupied with the thought of the remaining sixty-four emails in my inbox.

"Don't you want to know what it says?" he prompts.

"Yes, sure!" I try to show a little more involvement in our conversation, though the word "Will" makes me feel uncomfortable and sad.

"The temple and residence have been left to Nobu and Junko," he starts off, and I feel a piece of rice cracker struggling to make its way down my throat.

"Nobu is not sure yet what they will do, but he wanted you to know that Mrs. Toda specifically asked for Sala's Room to remain available to you for as long as you want."

"Okay …" I answer after a few concentrated last bites of a chocolate bar, suddenly feeling an odd queasiness toward the words "Sala's Room," and turn back to my laptop.

Yuki remains in place a few silent moments before adding, "Nobu stopped by the temple today to take Dharma so that you don't have to worry for him."

I rip open another chocolate bar.

Once Yuki realizes that I'm not planning to take part in this conversation, he softly excuses himself and goes back to his desk.

I leave the office a little before midnight, forty-eight unread emails still in my inbox. The subway home is packed with more drunken men than I have encountered in a while. Luckily, I am wearing my high heels, so I am at least a head higher than most of the alcohol fumes floating around. Relieved to reach my home station, I quickly make my way out into the open air.

When I arrive at the temple, I find a sign on the gate

stating that the temple will be closed until further notice.

The pain in the center of my chest grows, while something else, the core of what has gotten me through long days at the office—that feeling that somehow I belong somewhere—feels as if it is drifting away. Dharma being taken from me has only enhanced that feeling of detachment.

I open the gate and drag myself to my room where I lay on my futon. It is kind of weird going through the temple, even a bit daunting considering all the spirits who have been called on to visit it these past few days. I try to avoid sinking into such thoughts that could keep me up all night, yet I can't seem to shake off that feeling of profound emptiness.

I am so tired I fall asleep in my work attire. At 3:00 a.m., I wake up, failing to fall back asleep. I sit on my futon and look around at the empty room. I feel the time may have come for me to leave Japan. I know there is nothing waiting for me back in New Jersey. I can't stop thinking that perhaps my mother was right; perhaps this is a sign that it is time to go home … for good.

I lay down again, trying to picture what life could be like back in the States. At some point, I fall asleep again with these thoughts.

At 6:30 a.m., my alarm clock goes off. I get up, grab my laptop, and book a flight back to the U.S. I feel as if I am preprogrammed.

When I arrive at the office, I ask for an urgent meeting with Mr. Hashimoto. At 10:30 a.m., I am called to his office where I inform him of my plan to leave. I confront him with full determination.

Mr. Hashimoto doesn't seem surprised and is quite

supportive of my decision. I'm a little taken aback by his unquestioning reaction and feel the blood suddenly rush to my face. But then, he continues and promises to immediately reinstate me if I ever want to return to Japan.

The week goes by, and during my hours at the office, things are as they would be any other day of the year.

The evenings are a bit tougher, especially when I enter the temple gate. When I can no longer tolerate the silence around me, I end up calling my mother, feeling miserable again, and then finally falling asleep.

On Saturday at noon, I walk over to the temple. Akira has been showing up faithfully every day at noon since the funeral to chant sutras and attend to the family altar, hosting now not only the ashes of his beloved teacher but also the ashes of the woman who shared his loss for almost six years.

I find him deeply engaged in his ritual in front of the family altars, so I sit down next to him, on my knees, Japanese-style, trying not to interfere as I wait for his service to end. On finishing the last chant, he turns around, bows, and greets me with a smile.

I hand him a letter to give to Nobu. Since the incident at the temple, Nobu and I haven't crossed paths. I figure it is more likely that Akira will eventually see him now that Nobu has inherited the temple and since Akira is around more frequently than before and in more normal hours than I am. I thank him in advance then politely excuse myself.

I read the letter over and over before taking it to the temple and handing it to Akira. I just wanted to make sure I didn't write anything that could cause Nobu any trouble.

In the letter, I thank Nobu and ask him to thank his wife

for all she has done for me. I inform him of my return to the U.S. Finally, I state that, on my departure, Sala's Room will be at their disposal, sending my best wishes to him, Junko, and to their two lovely, little daughters.

As soon as I hand Akira the letter, I feel a sense of relief. Now I can finally allow myself to close the Japan chapter of my life, no strings attached, no regrets. After all, I've lived my dream. I have worn all the executive suits I could ever have dreamed of wearing and made my way up the corporate ladder to full independence in Japan, no regrets, no stone unturned. I'm finally ready to look in the mirror and to picture the *new me*. Just … this time targeting maternity wear instead of business suits, light yet stylish. Nothing too baggy.

Pastels will do nicely.

Chapter 34: Leaving Stuff Behind

I finish packing most of my belongings and take a few steps back to look around at the nearly empty space. Aside for some clothes that I've left out in the corner, there is still the big, white, fluffy carpet in the center of the room. *I will ask Yuki to take care of the carpet*, I conclude, much in the same way I've offloaded on him most of the uncomfortable issues of the last few weeks ... or months.

I scan the room truly for the last time, unable to take my eyes off my much-loved carpet. I recall the odd yet fatalistic day in which I first arrived with it at the temple after exiling it from Ben and my flat. I can't help but think how magical it has been to have had this singing angel looking out for me, even that rainy day. Truth is, I kind of regret never asking Mrs. Toda how she knew I'd be back in my room one day. Then again, maybe it was meant to remain a mystery, a legend. I feel my eyes fill with tears suddenly and decide to retreat toward my future. I back up slowly out of the door.

"Ow!" a familiar voice yelps as I skillfully manage to step on a toe in the doorway.

"*Gomennasai!*" I apologize, slowly turning around with

a hunch whose toe it was. *Typical! Landing on him again, at any given chance.*

"No, I am the one who is sorry," Nobu answers.

I gingerly look into his eyes.

"My wife died—"

"Oh no!" My heart skips a beat. "What? When? How …?" I continue before he can finish his sentence.

"When Izumi was born," he finally adds.

"What? Wait … I don't understand," I say as if we are speaking different languages.

"Junko is my sister. She is not my wife. I assumed you knew. Only when reading your letter, I understood you did not. She lives with us to help me with the girls and our father, who is growing older."

I feel my cheeks turn so red that I am sure they will soon burn in flames. "Oh my God! I … I slapped you in the face at Mrs. Toda's funeral. I was sure—"

"I drank too much. I hate funerals," Nobu quickly replies.

There is silence.

"You are sorry you slapped me?" Nobu suddenly asks, the smile returning to his eyes as he notes my regret.

I slowly drop my hands from my face, and I smile back at him, feeling the return of that special connection seasoned with flirtations.

We stare wordlessly into each other's eyes, and then he runs his cool hand through my hair and soon touches my lips, and I want more. I want to surrender.

I embrace his waist then run my fingertips over his well-built back, inch by inch. Then a sudden flash of reality hits me, and I recall that I am standing in my nearly empty room, almost fully packed.

It is too late. I am going back home to the States. I have the rest of my life planned out. I'm going to have a baby ... Well, at least I have potential plans ... my mother has plans ...

I am conflicted by my desire to give in and the understanding that things have changed, and I have made some major decisions lately.

Finally, I run my hands over to and up his chest, pushing him back gently, gradually creating some space between us. Then I step back, and my eyes turn cold and blank, and then I turn once more to look at the nearly empty room. "I thought I would leave the carpet here," I break the silence, shifting my empty gaze back at him.

"That is fine, if you want." Nobu's eyes mirror my withdrawal, and the air in the room thickens.

"I should leave," I say, looking at him in silence with nothing appropriate to add.

Nobu remains silent, as well, his eyes fixed on the ground. He nods toward me to signal that he understands then puts on the smallest smile he can gather. "*Mata ne*," he mumbles, the casual Japanese equivalent to "see ya," then turns and heads out in the direction of the temple.

My eyes follow him as he walks down the long corridor. I step into the room again, close the sliding door, and fall to my knees. My heart is racing, my eyes are dry, and my teeth are biting hard into my lips, trying to keep myself from slipping deep into a chaos of emotions. I am confused, sad, longing, and scared.

There is a knock at the door, and I leap to slide the door

open, closing my eyes and hoping …

"Sala-san? Are you okay?"

My eyes fly open in alarm. *Yuki!*

"Sleep on the plane tomorrow. You can't be tired today. Today, you are going to enjoy the best party in Tokyo," Yuki says cheerfully as he picks up my bags from the center of my room, stacking them in the corner.

I completely forgot about the farewell party that Yuki planned for me with the whole division.

I left some comfy clothes unpacked for the flight, together with three dresses so that Yuki can choose one for me, since he insisted that I wear one for the party.

I can't remember when I last wore a dress. Maybe at Noah and Rachel's wedding? But even that I'm not really sure of.

Yuki chooses one and, having come prepared to give me a full makeover, he sits me down on the *tatami* and opens up a small suitcase he brought with him. First, he powders my face like a good Japanese girl, and then he fixes me with some matching makeup, jewelry and, regrettably, one of those royal Japanese hairstyles.

In the entrance hall, Yuki bends down and slips my most elegant high heels onto my feet. Then, like a true gentleman, he accompanies me down the temple deck steps, along the pebble path, and out of the gate to a waiting taxi.

Chapter 35: Goodbyes

It has been a while since I last sat in a taxi during the early evening hours, looking out at Tokyo's nightlife, no agenda, no clients, and no deal to close. It is a crisp, clear evening, and the streetlights look bright and festive.

The taxi stops in front of a tall, white building in the Akasaka area where I've been endless times with endless clients. But I'm not familiar with a venue in this particular building.

As we step into the glossy, white lobby, a young Japanese woman in uniform greets us and accompanies us to the elevator. She enters the elevator with us and presses the top floor button.

Wake up! You are on your way to your own farewell party! I poke at myself frantically.

I am suddenly nervous.

Yuki, sensing my tension, smiles at me calmly and fixes my necklace. I smile back at him.

The elevator reaches the top floor. At first glance, the place looks as if aliens discovered both vintage and sushi and thought they would go nicely together. Tokyo's skyline surrounds us from all angles, making it look as if we are either in a rooftop aquarium or a spaceship. In the center of the room is a rotating sushi bar, almost transparent and mirroring the skyline around us so that the plates seem to be spinning on air.

Above the dining area, there is an elevated, round stage with a spotlight, the kind on which superheroes suddenly appear on and are transformed into their magical selves, making the karaoke singers look like holograms. The only solid thing is a selection of enormous antique armchairs that look as if they have been taken from a castle belonging to the Swedish royal family.

"Only in Japan," I mumble, unable to shift my gaze from the supernatural setting around us.

The members of my division stand in line and greet me as I pass them one by one. While I'm subsumed by the exquisite setting, the others seem to be taken with my complete makeover. No longer the business-suited, curry-eating, number-crunching boss, I am now as close to looking like a *real* woman in their eyes as they could have ever imagined.

Mr. Kobayashi greets me with a hug, which I find a little unsettling at first, but it eventually nearly makes me cry. Mr. Hashimoto shakes my hand warmly and follows me attentively with his smart, fatherly eyes as I am greeted by all the others.

I cannot help but wonder whether he is sad that he's losing me or proud that I'm moving on. I am seated between Mr. Hashimoto and Mr. Kobayashi, and I am treated like a galactic queen. I couldn't have asked for a warmer, more complimentary farewell.

Champagne and sushi are the theme, and what a perfect combination! Everyone seems to be enjoying themselves. For me, however, the most unexpected and entertaining moment of the whole evening is when Silent Rie goes up on stage and, without warning, unearths the voice of an angel.

So that is what Rie sounds like, I text Yuki under the table. He glances at his cell phone without missing a beat and grins.

As the evening continues, my mind shifts in and out of parallel universes. My thoughts are with Nobu, my body is at a magnificent party, and my soul is lost in space.

I am so relieved to discover that Nobu is not the uncaring, treacherous asshole that I took him for. And the more I think of him, the more I want to be close to him, as close as we were on the rice planting day. As close as we were today. I want to kiss him and to feel his soft, smooth chest against mine.

"Sala-san!" I hear Mr. Hashimoto calling me from the stage, catching me off guard.

Okay, so here are my final words of advice. In Japan, a lack of talent does not excuse you from always doing your best. After nearly fifteen years of successfully avoiding the center stage at the ubiquitous karaoke sessions, the time has finally come, and refusing Mr. Hashimoto is not an option. So, this is where the glory lies. Go the extra mile and sing a song in Japanese. They will love you for your efforts alone, even if you have a horrible voice, sing off key, and have absolutely no flair on stage, like me. So, here I go …

The next thing I know, I am waking up, still dressed like a princess. I have no idea when and how I got back to my room at the temple. A wicked hangover suggests that I maybe had just a little too much to drink.

I pull the blanket over my head, but before I can pass out again, I hear someone knocking on the door. At first, I try to ignore it somehow. With the hangover and all, I cannot imagine getting out of bed. But after a few persistent knocks, I finally give in.

Yuki is standing at the door, smiling.

"What time is it?" I ask, dragging myself back to my futon, one eye half-open.

"You better get dressed. It is almost time to leave," Yuki answers, standing above me, flashing his cell phone to show me the time.

Oh my God! It is close to noon, and I have a train to catch to the airport.

My head is pounding and the dress is so uncomfortable.

Yuki stands there, looking amused. I imagine it is my hairstyle that is entertaining him, but in my state, it could be anything.

I turn around and point at the impossible zipper of my dress, recalling why I slept in it in the first place. Then I hurry to the bathroom to get washed up.

I burst out laughing at the sight of my uncensored hairdo—Madam Medusa.

When I get back to the room, Yuki is waiting for me with a can of coffee that he brought back from the convenience store. I slurp the coffee down, popping two Advils.

"So, this is it?" I ask.

He smiles at me and says he will take me back as his boss any time, but he would have to insist on a raise. We both smile sadly at each other.

"I'll certainly miss hot coffee from a can," I say as I eke out that last drop, which always leaves me wanting more.

We head out, and at the gate, I turn back and look at the temple one more time. I can almost see Mrs. Toda sitting there, birthday hat above her sweet grey bangs, smiling and waving goodbye.

"I can't," I hear myself say out loud, avoiding Yuki's attempts to get me moving as I stand in place, staring blankly at the temple.

"You will miss your flight," I hear him say again as I snap back into reality.

"There is something I need to …" I call out to him without even turning his way, my eyes still locked on the temple deck.

I drop the fake Louis Vuitton bag hanging over my shoulder and my bright pink carry-on suitcase from my recently purchased set of matching suitcases, and I run toward the empty temple. I feel a strong rush of clarity as I remove my shoes, climb up the deck, and rush down the wooden corridor and into the kitchen. But as I enter the kitchen, the clarity all fades away. *What was I looking for?*

I stare blankly at the empty kitchen. *The beer bottle opener!* Clarity suddenly returns, and I head across the kitchen, removing the bottle opener from its hanger.

"*Some Things Taste Better with Time*," I read the inscription to myself as I hold the beer opener in my hand. It is the only actual physical reminder I can take with me from an experience that changed my life completely. My refuge at Mrs. Toda's temple helped me define who I want to be.

"If only …" I mumble to myself as my mind starts

spinning and anxiety takes over.

"If only what?" a deep voice calls out from behind me.

I freeze in place, my heart beating stronger than before. Then I feel his warm hand land on my shoulder, and I shut my eyes. I am terrified.

I turn to Nobu and fall into his embracing arms. He kisses me gently on my head, hugging me so close. I feel safe.

"You won't catch your flight if you don't leave now," he whispers in my ear, holding me even tighter.

"Excuse me, Sala; we have to go," I hear Yuki call out from the kitchen entrance.

I stare beyond Nobu's wide shoulders, hoping Yuki can see in my eyes my deep, sincere gratitude for all he's done for me. "I know. It's okay …" I say, hearing how Japanese I sound, not being explicit while communicating with minimal discomfort.

Yuki excuses himself, as if reading my mind.

I let out a tiny wink, which he happily catches before he disappears behind the kitchen entrance.

"I am not leaving," I whisper back into Nobu's ear. I then stare into his eyes, feeling his reassurance.

His eyes are darker than I have ever seen them, and shiny, like black pebbles in silent seas. I dive into them softly, recognizing how much I need him.

I kiss him gently on his lips and run my fingers over his hard, strong back. I can feel his shoulders. Oh … how I love men's shoulders. I slowly pull up his black Polo shirt, running my hands over his smooth, carved chest. He grabs me with both hands and lifts me up into his arms.

"Once again, I carry you to your room," he says

charmingly, teasing me about the time I passed out on the pebble path leading to Mrs. Toda's temple.

I find myself smiling at him with the widest smile I have shown in years.

He opens the sliding door of my room and gently sets me down on my feet.

I look around the room and realize Mrs. Toda had it all figured out.

The white, fluffy carpet is spread out in the center of the room. The same carpet I imagined Ben and I laying on, making angels with our hands and feet like kids in the snow. *I guess I just missed the point back then*, I tell myself, amused by the thought. *I guess it was meant for me and Nobu, my angel himself.*

I let out a small giggle as Nobu places himself on the fluffy carpet beside me. I pull him toward me, and he runs his lips over my neck. *It's been so long since I actually felt loved* ... He positions me carefully on my back and runs his fingers through my hair, simply staring into my eyes. *Could Mrs. Toda have known back on that rainy day that I would need the carpet to save me from the cold, hard tatami floors while making love to Nobu? Or was it her conspiracy with the Japanese spirits?*

With his manly hands, Nobu opens my top, button by button. I can feel his warmth over me, and I surrender as every inch of me uncontrollably absorbs his longed-for touch.

Chapter 36: Pickled Plums

G-O-N-G. It is 5:00 a.m., and the gong is struck for the first time.

G-O-N-G. And again.

G-O-N-G. It goes off once more.

Akira! I cry out in my head.

Akira wakes up the temple guests for morning meditation, which is part of the deal.

I take a deep breath and try to accept my fate. I am, after all, living on the grounds of a Buddhist temple.

I feel a kick from inside me and the weight of a large hand on my belly.

I close my eyes and am suffused with that sense of peace and security that I have always longed for. I'm in his arms, the arms of the man who made perfect love to me just a few hours ago.

I am so tired.

At 8:00 a.m., I'm woken up with the warmest, most precious hugs. Hiromi and Izumi are both leaning their heads on my chest, their soft, silky hair brushing my face, and their little arms wrapped as far around me as they can manage. I am filled with joy, the kind of joy I've never felt before.

I open my eyes to Izumi's bright smile. Nobu knows I cannot resist them and has been using them as ammunition to get me moving on those days when I feel so exhausted from the pregnancy that I would rather stay in bed all day.

Before I can get my foot into the second slipper, the girls have dragged me through the corridor and into the dining room.

Dharma soon joins us.

Okay, so you probably want to know how it all happened.

Apparently, in my heavily intoxicated state on the ride home from my farewell party, I told Yuki everything—Nobu kissing me, slapping him in return, the letter, Junko, the dead wife … And Yuki, being the romantic he is, called Nobu first thing on the morning of my flight, giving him one last chance to be my hero. The moment Nobu hugged me, I had no doubt that I belonged with him.

A few weeks after my missed flight, I rebooked a short trip to the States. When I returned, Nobu and I moved in together, with the girls, into the temple grounds. Shortly after, I got pregnant and decided not to go back to my firm. Instead, I set up a Buddhist meditation center on the temple grounds, with Nobu's and Junko's blessings, hoping to help others take the time to consider their priorities in life, knowing firsthand that running a career in Tokyo has a high personal price.

The girls and I sit down at the knee-high table and wait in anticipation for the man of the house. A fire is lit in the traditional fireplace in the center of the dining space, and the crackling of the wood surrendering to the hungry flames sparks my own hunger.

"*Some Things Taste Better with Time*," I read the words on the bottle opener. Nobu must have left it on the table last night after dinner when we had some private time together. He enjoyed a bottle of Asahi beer while I ate my usual Japanese hot fudge sundae, resembling tofu with soy sauce and ginger.

Nobu appears before us, and the four of us turn our heads, Dharma included, of course. Nobu stands there, a tray in his strong, reassuring hands.

I am finally home, I think to myself as Nobu sits himself on the cushion next to me, handing out the food, which is nicely laid out on the tray.

"*Itadakimasu*," we say together then quietly sip the miso soup, pick up our chopsticks, and decorate our rice with salty and sour, homemade, Japanese pickled plums.

About the Author

This is Ruth Reiner's first novel. Her special connection with both Japan and with writing started at a young age. Her love of Japan was triggered by her love of Japanese *Koto* music, after receiving a cassette tape, which her father had brought back from one of his many business travels abroad. She self-published a booklet of poems at the age of nine. One of her poems, about *peace*, even grabbed the attention of a later-selected Nobel Prize Winner.

Many aspects of the book are based on her own life story. At the age of twenty-four, she was invited to spend one year with the Japanese Shinto community, "Oomoto," living on the grounds of their Shinto shrine, in Kameoka, a city in the countryside of Kyoto. Ruth holds a Japan-focused MBA from the University of Hawaii and The Japan-American Institute of Management Science. Following her studies, she spent a decade leading business negotiations between Japanese and non-Japanese firms. At the age of thirty-nine, Ruth had her first, and so far only, child, the light and love of her life and the inspiration for writing this novel.

ENJOYED?
DON'T FORGET TO LEAVE A REVIEW!

Link to review on Amazon
amazon.com/dp/B08PW6QP6Y

Link to review on Goodreads
goodreads.com/book/show/55989687

Want to be notified when my next book is out?
Leave a message on my website
reiner-ruth.com

Follow me on Facebook
facebook.com/RuthReinerBooks

Follow me on Twitter
twitter.com/ReinerRuth

Made in the USA
Monee, IL
12 June 2021